MESSENGER
PAUL TOBIN
RAY NADINE

Rocketship™

rocketshipent.com

Tom Akel, CEO & Publisher • **Rob Feldman,** CTO • **Jeanmarie McNeely,** CFO
Brandon Freeberg, VP, Production & Partner Relations • **Aram Alekyan,** Designer
Jimmy Deoquino, Producer • **Jed Keith,** Social Media • **Jerrod Clark,** Publicity

MESSENGER VOLUME 1 | Hardcover ISBN: 978-1-962298-10-0 | Softcover ISBN: 978-1-962298-09-4
First printing. May 2024. Published by Rocketship Entertainment, LLC. 136 Westbury Court. Doylestown, PA 18901. Printed in China.

For this edition, production and supplemental design by **Phil Smith**

TABLE OF CONTENTS

RADIO

CHAPTER 1

NYOOOM!!
ONE WAY
STAR CLIPPER!
GRAND OPENING!
BIG D
HAULS
BIG DUDE HAUL STUFF
RNW
NGERY
THE COAT HANGERS

4:12

FLOWERAMA!

BELL
RING! RING!

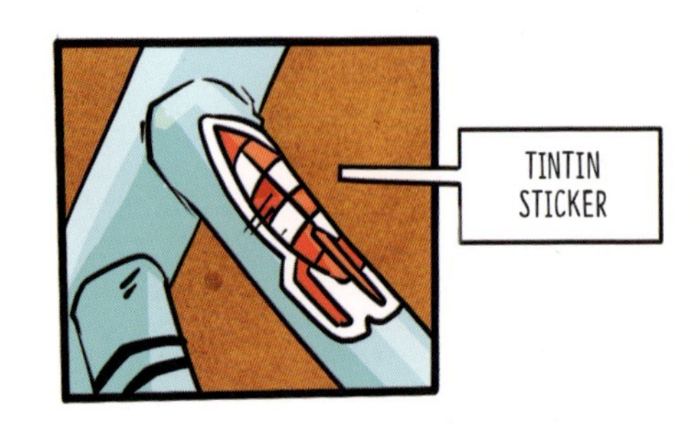
TINTIN STICKER

KARAOKE MACHINE
ITS FRIDAY, IM IN LOVE SATURDAY

3:15
PHONE CLIP

STEINBERG "LEOPARD FIRE-X" CONVERSION FIXIE BIKE
NICKNAMED "GRETA"

DARE CRILLEY,
BIKE MESSENGER
22 YEARS OLD,
5'5" 124 LBS
SCORPIO
CHEW!
...AND SO YOU BROKE UP WITH HIM?
LULU DEL CARMEN,
BEST FRIEND
NOT SURE. MAYBE HE BROKE UP WITH ME?
IT WAS KINDA CHAOTIC.
REALLY? DID YOU USE GRENADES? WERE THE POLICE CALLED? THE ARMY?!

IT WAS A... COLD CHAOS
WE HAD A FEW DRINKS AND JUST
GLARED AT EACH OTHER

WELL, GOOD THING I HAVE AT LEAST ELEVEN FRIENDS I CAN HOOK YOU UP WITH.

THERE'S NILE, BENJAMIN, TYLER,

INSTAPIX

the_nile
IT guy. Foodie. INTP.

benJAMMIN13
party on my dudes

life_of_ty
Guitar is life. Music is love.

jujubee
travellin' and living! <3

dan_chan1216
Aspiring photog. Taurus.

mary.andrews
mom, artist, dreamer.

HIROHIRO
keep sk8in

JUJU, DAN-CHAN, MARY, HIROSHI...

WE'RE PETTING YOUR DOG!
SOON...
CHUM C
LOOK! MY BIKE STORE COULD GO RIGHT HERE.
CHUM-CHUM Café
CHUMCHUM
Closed
FOR RENT
CALL: 555-326-0157 SAMWELL REALTY

THIS IS JUST THE OLD CHUM-CHUM CAFE.
TAP! TAP!
WHICH MEANS IT'S GOT A KITCHEN.
YOU DON'T NEED A KITCHEN FOR A BIKE STORE.
FOR FEAR!

AND HOW ARE YOUR SAVINGS, ANYWAY?
GOT ENOUGH FOR A STORE?
I NEED A QUARTER MILLION FOR START-UP, AND I'VE GOT... ALMOST TWO THOUSAND.
OUCH!
BODY BLOW!

DARE CRILLEY VERSUS BANK ACCOUNT!
ROUND ONE!
KNOCKOUT!
CHUM-
Café
Closed
YOU'RE HELPING SO MUCH RIGHT NOW.
I DO WHAT I CAN.
3:51p

UM-CHUM
Café
~SIGH~
Oscar Wilde

!!
TURN!!

HUH? NOBODY?
WHAT'S UP?
CHUM-CHUM CAFÉ
FOR RENT
WHOOSH!

JUST THOUGHT I SAW A REFLECTION.
IT WAS PROBABLY YOU AS AN OLD MAID.

LET'S GET BACK ON TRACK!

SO THERE'S...
HIROSHI

AND...
RAFE

AND RAFE'S SISTER...
MOTORPOOL

YOU HAVE A FRIEND NAMED MOTORPOOL? THAT'S-
FOR FEARS

RING RING!
ANSWER!

DARE? THERE'S AN URGENT PICKUP AT THE GILBERTON BUILDING AND YOUR GPS SAYS YOU'RE CLOSE.
COULD YOU...?
ON IT!
SOON...
PICKUP?
OH, GOOD! YOU'RE HERE!
WE ONLY HAVE TWELVE MINUTES!
PLEASE HURRY!
NO PROBLEM!
I'M THE BEST.

COO-

THE BEST, HUH?

WE'LL SEE ABOUT THAT
CAW!
CAW!

!

CHAPTER 2

6:29

BUZZ BUZZ BLARE
SNOOZE
SET
6:30
AM

GAH!
BUZZ BUZZ BUZZ
HSSST!

OUT OF THE WAY, SMIRKLEY!
HAVE TO PEEEEEEE!

BATHROOM! TOILET!
QUIT LOOKING AT ME!

BATHROOM! SHOWER!
THUNDER BOLT AND LIGHTNING
VERY VERY FRIGHTENING ME!
GALLILEOoooooo
MAGNIFICO OH - OH - OH!
QUEEN
(SORT OF)

GLARE

ACTUALLY BRUSHING TEETH!
PRETENDING TO COMB HAIR!
FALCON
NEW HOWL

CLOTHES, CLOTHES, CLOTHES!
?

GOTTA GET DRESSED, DRESSED, DRESSED!
TOSS!
REACH!
-YAWN!
DARE

OKAY, SMIRKLEY!
PLEASE KEEP YOUR MONSTROUS DESTRUCTION, HAIRBALLS, AND RANDOM PUKING TO A MINIMUM TODAY.

MY STEED!

WE RIDE!

HI, DARE!
MORNING MR. COFFEE KING!
fresh Coffee
MACS
BLM

HELLO DARE!
RAMP SOMETHING!
SHE CAN'T ALWAYS BE RAMPING EVERYTHING.
IT'S NOT SAFE TO-

WAHHH-HOOOO!!!
RAMP!

SORRY!
DIDN'T MEAN TO GIVE HER ANY BAD IDEAS!

RING RING RING
LULU !!
ANSWER

HELLO? DARE!
IT'S LULU.

COME OVER LATER! WE'RE DOING MOVIE NIGHT!
Cakes!

WE'LL BE WATCHING CABARET. YOU KNOW, THE BURLESQUE ONE.
EXTRA POINTS IF YOU DRESS UP!

YOU'RE TRING TO SET ME UP WITH SOMEONE, AREN'T YOU?
EXTRA POINTS FOR FIGURING THAT OUT!

SO, CAN YOU MAKE IT?

TWO MESSENGERS ARE OUT SICK TODAY SO I'M WORKING DOUBLE DELIVERIES.
I'D PROBABLY JUST FALL ASLEEP ON YOUR COUCH.
SPEED 25

MAYBE WE COULD WATCH *SLEEPING BEAUTY* INSTEAD.
THEN YOU'D BE LIKE, A PERFORMANCE PIECE.

WHAT'D SHE SAY?
THAT SHE'LL ABSOLUTELY BE THERE AND TOTALLY WANTS TO MEET YOU.

WHO WERE YOU JUST TALKING TO?
UHH... I... I'M ON A BUS. YOU MUST HAVE HEARD SOMEONE ELSE.

BOOP! BEEP!
GOTTA GO! I'M GETTING CRUSHED!
GONNA TURN ON THE KARAOKE AND REVISIT THE DISCO ERA!
I PITY THOSE WHO HEAR YOU. AND I BETTER SEE YOU LATER!

OOH YEAH!
WHETHER YOU'RE A BROTHER OR A MOTHER!
OH YEAH! DO DO DOOOO!
STAYIN' ALIIIIIVE!
BEE GEES (SORT OF)
MOVIES
10:29 A.M.
NEED IT THERE IN TEN MINUTES!
10:48 A.M.
DARE! WE NEED YOU AT THE OFFICES OF LEVINSON AND LIEBER
THEY HAVE SIX PACKAGES FOR IMMEDIATE DELIVERY!
ONE WAY!

11:20 A.M.
BAILEY'S BAIL BONDS
OPEN!
Floral
GET A SIGNATURE AND BRING IT BACK!
NEED THAT IN COURT IN THIRTY MINUTES! GO!

SO, SHE'S PRETTY?
IF YOU'RE SHALLOW AND THAT'S WHAT YOU WANT TO FOCUS ON, THEN YES... SHE'S GORGEOUS.
BUT SHE'S MORE THAN JUST PRETTY.
SHE'S **DARE CRILLEY.**
SHE'S A LEGEND, BECAUSE IN EIGHT YEARS SHE'S *NEVER* MISSED A DELIVERY

SHE'LL JUMP BRIDGES
OR PEDAL THROUGH RIOTS, HURRICANES,
AND BLIZZARDS
CR-ACK!

NO MATTER WHAT,
NOTHING STOPS DARE
FROM DELIVERING
KHH-KRASSHH!

I'M ALREADY HALF-WAY IN LOVE.
WELL THEN, YOU'RE ONLY HALF-WAY SMART.

ELSEWHERE...
BOSS, YOU SAID IT WAS APARTMENT SIX, RIGHT?
YEP. NEW CLIENT WHO PAID IN ADVANCE.
MENTIONED HE MIGHT NEED REGULAR HELP, SO IMPRESS HIM!
4

OKAY!
6
KNOCK KNOCK!

SHE'S HERE.
GIVE ME A
KNOCK KNOCK

KNOCK KNOCK KNOCK!

CLICK!

CHAPTER 3

6
CREEEAK!

HI! DARE CRILLEY, FOR DYNASTY DELIVERY. I'M HERE TO PICK UP-
THIS NEEDS TO BE AT HELIOSCOPE STUDIO ON FIFTH AVENUE IN SEVEN MINUTES.

BLINK!
BLINK!

GRAB!

RUN RUN RUN!
LEAP!

FWUMPP!

RUN RUN RUN RUN RUN

ONE WAY
GRETA!

WE RIDE!

SPLASH!
SPLISH!
RUN RUN

RAMP!
OH!

ARF!
BOOF!
GRRR-RUFF!
BARK BARK!

RUFF?
SORRY, MADAME TICKBAIT! I'LL TAKE YOU BACK IN A MINUTE!

HELIOSCOPE DR
FIFTH AVE
RUN RUN RUN

HERE!
A DELIVERY FOR-

HUH? IT'S YOU?
HOW'D YOU GET HERE SO FAST?

I TOOK SHORTCUTS.

BUT YOU DIDN'T, AND YOU STILL MADE IT IN TIME. IT WAS... HMM.
?

THIS IS UNSETTLING. IRRITATING, EVEN.

I HAVE TO GO CONSULT WITH MY COLLEAGUES.
WAIT HERE, PLEASE.

I TOLD YOU SHE WAS FAST.

CAN SHE DO IT?
WE HAVE TO TRY.
DO WE NEED TO RUSH INTO THIS?
WE'RE GODS, NOT COWARDS.
LET'S GIVE HER A CHANCE.
ALL THE OTHERS WERE SLOW OR AFRAID. DID YOU SEE THAT RAMP?
I LIKE HER SINGING VOICE. NOT EVERYONE CAN HANDLE THE BEE-GEES.

I DON'T LIKE THIS. SHE'S FULL OF HERSELF. SHE'S **HUMAN.**
WE DON'T NEED HER.
SHE MADE THE DELIVERY, JUNG.
I UNDERSTAND WHY YOU HAVE PROBLEMS WITH HUMANS.
BUT JUNG... WE HAVE BIGGER PROBLEMS RIGHT NOW.

AND SHE MADE THE DELIVERY

TAP!
TAP!

CLICK!
??

OKAY, THEY'RE ALL OFFICIALLY IMPRESSED. I HATE THIS, BUT...
...I THINK YOU GET THE JOB.

AND WHAT JOB IS THAT?
DELIVERING PACKAGES? KINDA ALREADY GOT THAT JOB.
I DON'T KNOW WHO YOU ARE OR WHY YOU KEPT ME WAITING-
MY NAME IS JUNG DARROW.
AND I GUESS YOU COULD CALL ME...

A GOD.
BLINK!
BLINK!

YOU'RE A WHAT NOW?

SHUNK!
FRONT DOOR SEAL.

WINDOWS BLACK.

PLEASE DON'T SCREAM.
THERE IS LITERALLY NO SENTENCE THAT WOULD MAKE ME MORE LIKELY TO SCREAM.

OPEN!
WALK WALK WALK

HELLO.

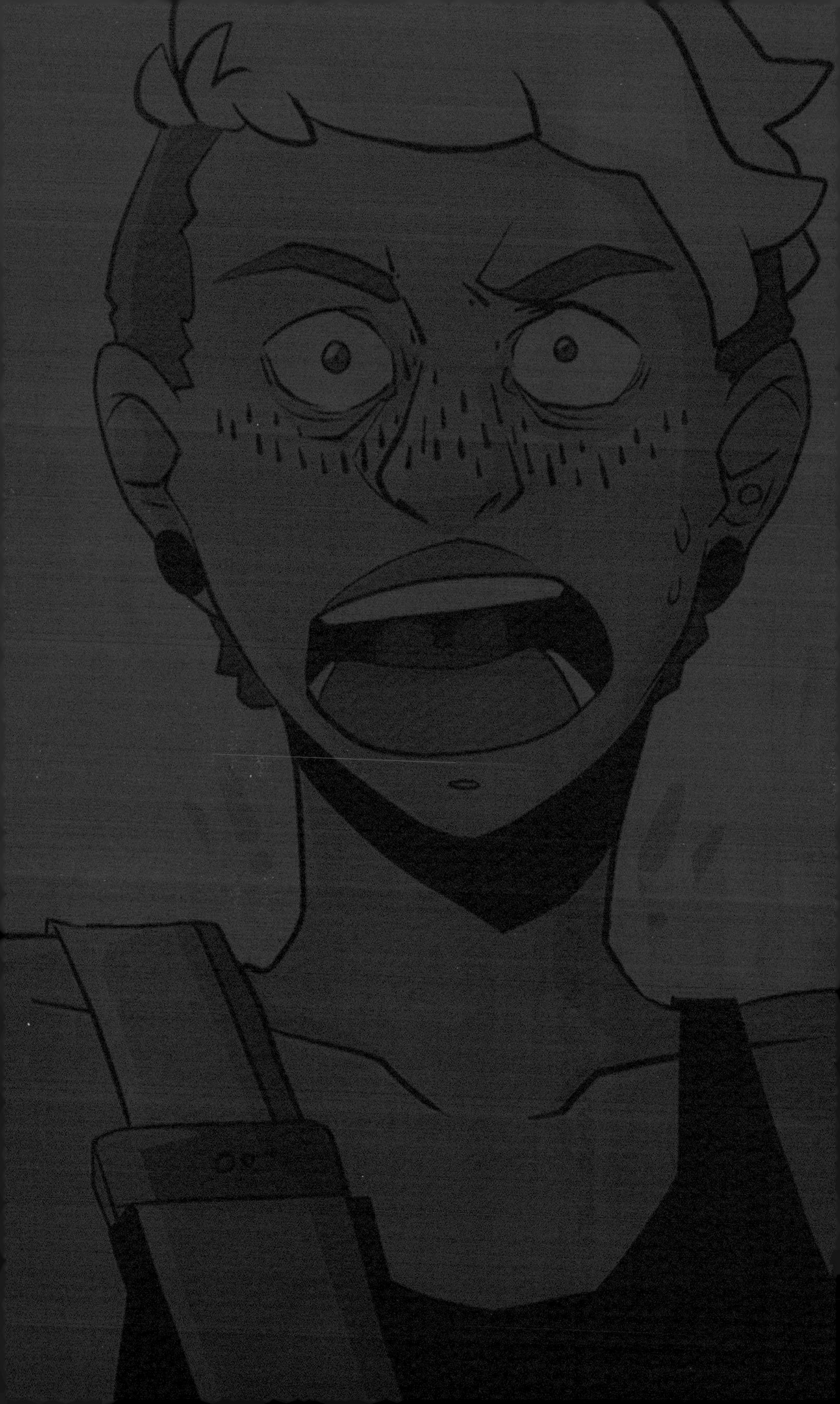

CHAPTER 4

LET ME FILL YOU IN ON SOME THINGS

THERE'S AN ENDLESS CITY IN AN ENDLESS WORLD WHERE ALL THE GODS RESIDE

THE CITY OF GERIK AND THE LAND OF FELDANA ARE BOTH FILLED WITH AN INCREDIBLE ARRAY OF GODS WHO ARE, FOR THE MOST PART, SEPARATED INTO THREE DISTINCT CATEGORIES
GERIK CITY
-TAP ROOM-

THERE'S THE GOOD

THE BAD

AND THE, EH, WHATEVER
ZZZ..
TAP TAP!

NO WAY. ADSOLUTELY NOT.
THIS IS CRAZY.

ARE YOU EVEN CLOSE TO SERIOUS?
I DON'T EVEN KNOW WHAT TO THINK.
AS I SAID, MY NAME IS JUNG. JUNG DARROW.
THE GOD OF CAFÉ NAPKINS.

WELL, THAT'S RATHER SPECIALIZED.

IT'S AN IMPORTANT JOB! WHAT IF YOU SPILL YOGURT ON YOUR PHONE?
WHAT IF YOU GET CREAM CHEESE ON YOUR LIPS AND THE CUTE BARISTA IS-

CALM DOWN, JUNG. I'M SURE SHE'S SUITABLY IMPRESSED.
NAPKINS, AFTER ALL.
VERY IMPORTAN

ANYWAY, DARE, WE KNOW IT'S A LOT TO TAKE IN.
JUST REMEMBER, DEEP BREATHS AND AN OPEN MIND.
OH, AND MY NAME IS TORGA.

I'M THE GOD OF INTERNET BROWSING HISTORY.
OH.

OH SHIT.

DON'T WORRY, I WON'T TELL ANYONE.
OH, THANK YOU!

HI, I'M BALTHANE. THE GOD OF UNSENT TEXT MESSAGES.

AND DOWN THERE IS PIBBS.
HE'S A GOD GUIDE.
HELLO, TALL PIG!

FIRST OF ALL, MY NAME IS DARE, NOT TALL PIG.
AND, YOU'RE A GUIDE? WHAT'S THAT MEAN?
IT MEANS I'LL BE ANSWERING ALL OF YOUR QUESTIONS AND GUIDING YOU THROUGH FELDANA.
NOBODY COULD POSSIBLY ANSWER ALL OF MY QUESTIONS.
AND WHY WOULD I BE GOING TO THE LAND OF THE GODS?

WAIT! AM I A GOD AND JUST DIDN'T KNOW IT?!

HARDLY. YOU COULD NEVER ASPIRE TO OUR HEIGHTS.

QUIT BEING SUCH AN ENORMOUS SNOTBALL, JUNG.
IT'S TIME WE LET HER KNOW WHAT'S GOING ON.

YOU SEE, THERE'S BEEN TROUBLE BREWING IN FELDANA RECENTLY. LIKE, FOR MAYBE THE LAST SIX OR SEVEN THOUSAND YEARS

MORE AND MORE, THE SEPARATE FACTIONS DON'T WANT TO TALK TO EACH OTHER. WE'RE BECOMING ISOLATIONIST. AND THAT'S CAUSING CATASTROPHIC PROBLEMS

I MEAN, NOT UNLESS YOU COUNT **"END OF ALL REALITY"** AS "END OF THE WORLD."
!

OOOH, I SUPPOSE WE SHOULD?
!
YEAH. I GUESS THAT'S TRUE.

I MEAN, THINK OF WHAT HAPPENS WHEN THE GOD OF PROTONS WON'T TALK TO THE GOD OF NEUTRONS! EVERYTHING LITERALLY FALLS APART

ANYWAY, SINCE NOBODY WILL TALK TO EACH OTHER. WHAT WE NEED...

...IS A MESSENGER

WE NEED YOU TO FERRY MESSAGES BACK AND FORTH BETWEEN THE GODS, REOPENING THOSE LINES OF COMMUNICATION

YOU'LL GET SOME GOLD EVERY TIME YOU COMPLETE A DELIVERY. ENOUGH TO EVENTUALLY OPEN THE BEST BIKE STORE IN THE UNIVERSE, IF YOU WANT TO

THERE'S ALSO A BONUS FOR EVERY SUCCESSFUL DELIVERY

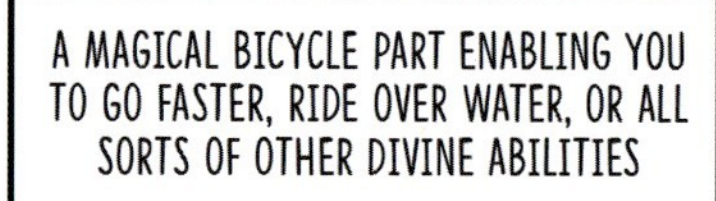

A MAGICAL BICYCLE PART ENABLING YOU TO GO FASTER, RIDE OVER WATER, OR ALL SORTS OF OTHER DIVINE ABILITIES

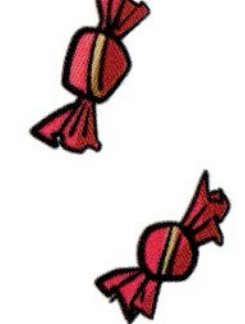

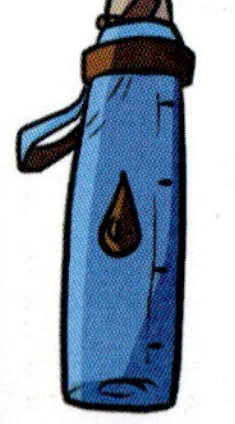

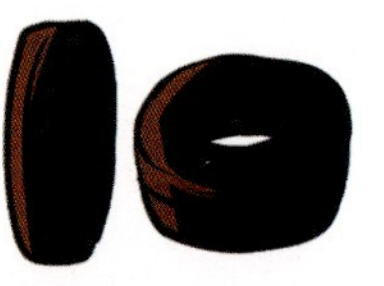

THIS BIKE ORN CREATES COOKIES. R POSSIBLY AN ACTIVE VOLCANO?
I'M NOT REALLY SURE WHICH.
ANYWAY, YOU WANT THE JOB OR NOT?

HONESTLY, THIS IS REALLY OVERWHELMING. YOU KEEP TALKING ABOUT WHAT HAPPENS IF I MAKE ONE OF THESE DELIVERIES...
...WHAT HAPPENS IF I FAIL?

DON'T FAIL ONE.
YEAH, THAT WOULD BE BAD.
HOW BAD?
...
LET'S JUST STICK WITH... DON'T FAIL ONE.
HEY! KNOW WHAT? I'M GONNA HONK THIS THING. SEE WHAT HAPPENS.

CHAPTER 5

CREATURE
BLUE LAKE
The BRIDE OF BIG MAN KARLON
THIS IS RIDICULOUS, LULU. I'M GOING TO DIE ALONE.
I'M GOING TO TURN TO RUST AND WITHER INTO TINY, BROKEN PIECES.
SHE'LL BE HERE, TOM.
KNOCK-KNOCK!
SEE? I BET THAT'S DARE RIGHT NOW!

HAH! IT'S DARE! DARE IS HERE!
HOW DID I GET HERE?

HI, DARE. MY NAME IS TOM. I WAS HOPING YOU'D-

YOUR ROOM.
IN PRIVATE.
NOW.

WHAT'S...? DARE! WHAT ARE YOU DOING?
DID SOMETHING HAPPEN?
AUDREY HEPBURN

AUGUST
SLAM!

WHAT IS GOING ON?!
I THINK I GOT A NEW JOB. I MET A WEIRD GUY...
...AND I'VE GONE CRAZY.

HUH?
BUT YOU ALREADY HAVE A JOB.
AND ALL GUYS ARE WEIRD!
PLUS YOU WERE ALREADY CRAZY!

HOW DID I GET HERE?

LULU? I'M SERIOUSLY WEIGHING THE FATE OF THE UNIVERSE, SO I NEED YOU TO BE TOTALLY HONEST.
AM I... GOOD AT DELIVERING?

DUH!
YOU'RE THE BEST EVER! THE UNDISPUTED WORLD CHAMPION, YOU'RE A LEGEND!

~SIGH~
WELL THEN, GUESS I'M GONNA DO THIS.
?
?
?
DO WHAT?
AUG
'02

DARE? DO WHAT?
HI! I'M TOM-
BRIDE OF BIG MAN
HOW DID
PBR

DARE!

DO WHAT?!

KNOCK! KNOCK! KNOCK!

FOREBODING ABYSS
(SOUNDS LIKE CATS HISSING)

SINISTER ABYSS
(SMELLS LIKE CINNAMON)
OMINOUS ABYSS
(FEELS LIKE CHEWED GUM)

HEY, DARE. JUNG'S NOT HERE RIGHT NOW,
PROBABLY FOR THE BEST, SEEING AS HE DOESN'T LIKE YOU.

I NOTICED.
WHAT'S UP WITH *THAT?*
OH, IT'S NOTHING PERSONAL. HE JUST HATES HUMANS IN GENERAL.
LONG STORY AND NOT MINE TO TELL.
I SUPPOSE YOU'RE HERE ABOUT THE JOB?

YEAH, I AM.

TAKING IT?
YEAH, TAKING IT.

FABULOUS. BUT WE HAVE TO GIVE YOU ONE MORE TEST BEFORE YOU QUALIFY.
YOU HAVE TO...
DIVINITY DROPS!
YUM!

Torga HP
...DEFEAT ME IN BATTLE.
Dare HP
>Fight >Item
>Run

PAP!

YEAH. GOOD ENOUGH.
I'M FEELING SUITABLY VANQUISHED

PIBBS! GET OUT HERE!

HELLO?
OH! IT'S TALL PIG! ARE YOU TAKING THE JOB?

SHE IS.
AND HER NAME'S **DARE SALT CRILLEY,** NOT TALL PIG.
THOOP!

RESPECT HER.
SHE'S RISKING ALMOST CERTAIN DEATH TAKING THIS JOB.

I'M **WHAT** NOW?

SO, YOU READY TO GO? I BROUGHT YOUR BIKE.

HOW'D YOU GET GRETA?! I LOCKED HER UP OUTSIDE!
NOT A BIG DEAL FOR ME. I JUST REACHED THROUGH SPACE-TIME. WARPED REALITY. TWISTED THE UNIVERSE. THAT SORT OF THING.

I AM DIVINE, YOU KNOW.

OH YEAH. GOD OF INTERNET BROWSING HISTORY.
CORRECT!

AKA, THE GOD OF KNOWING ALL THE WEIRD STUFF ABOUT EVERYBODY.
ANYWAY, GET ON YOUR BIKE.

WOAH, WHAT'S THAT?

IT'S TIME TO RIDE!
SHOVE!

DID
I
GET
HERE?

CHAPTER 6

HUH?
WHOA!

IT'S REALLY TRUE? THIS IS FELDANA?
THE LAND OF THE GODS?

YEP. IT'S TRUE. ALSO, YOU SHOULD DUCK.

WHAPP!
ACK!
FLOPP!
OOF!
FLOOP!
GAHH!

HOOT!
S & EYES!
CRASH!
YOU SPILLED MY EYEBALLS! AND THESE PISTACHIOS!
NUTS & EYES!
NUTS
SORRY!
IT'S NOT MY FAULT! I WAS-
WHOOSH!
WHOA!
WHAT THE HECK?!
WHIFF!

IT'S AN OBSTACLE GOD.
STOP!
WALL

I COULD EXPLAIN ALL ABOUT OBSTACLE GODS, OR... YOU COULD TRY TO ESCAPE.
YOUR CHOICE!

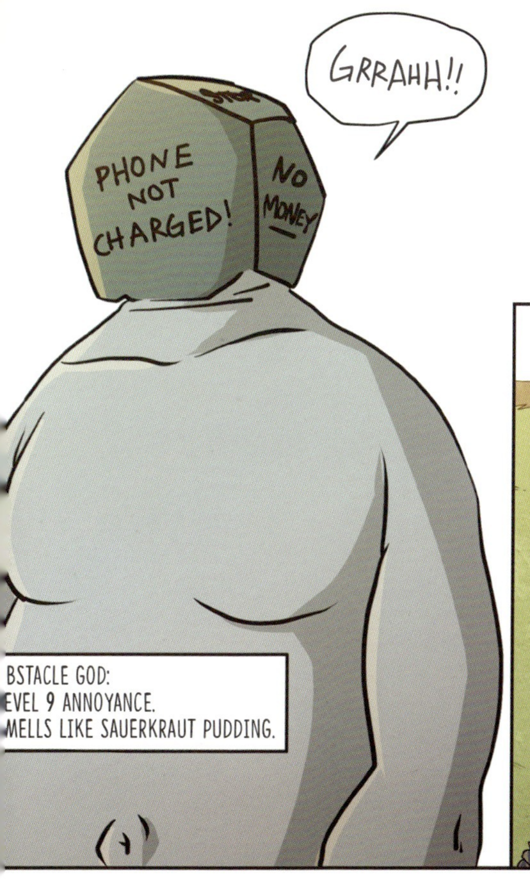
GRRAHH!!
PHONE NOT CHARGED!
NO MONEY
BSTACLE GOD:
EVEL 9 ANNOYANCE.
MELLS LIKE SAUERKRAUT PUDDING.

ESCAPE NOW!
LEARN LATER!
WISE CHOICE! HERE'S YOUR BIKE. I WOULD ADVISE NOT FALLING OFF ANYMORE, IT COULD GET STOLEN.

AFTER ALL, THERE ARE SEVENTEEN DIFFERENT VARIETIES OF THIEF GODS IN RESIDENCE.

WHAT? WHY ARE THERE SO MANY-

GONNNG!

OOOO, DELIVERY REQUEST! YOU NEED TO GET THIS.
NOW IS **NOT** A GOOD TIME!

HA HA HA! I'LL ASSUME YOU'RE MAKING A JOKE. THERE'S NO SUCH THING AS GOOD TIMES AND BAD TIMES FOR YOU ANYMORE.
THERE'S ONLY DELIVERY TIMES, AND NOT DELIVERY TIMES.

THAT'S NOT FAIR!
WELL, I SUPPOSE YOU COULD COMPLAIN TO THE GOD OF BEING FAIR, BUT SHE'S DRUNK RIGHT NOW.

HAHA! I THINK ABOUT FARTING A LOT! HAHA!
SOBER
WASTED!

OKAY.
OH MAN.
THIS WORLD.

GAHHH!
WHOOSH!

IT SAYS I'M SUPPOSED TO PICK UP A PACKAGE AT ***PEACHTREE POINT.***
WHERE'S THAT?

FOLLOW ME! UNTIL YOU LEARN THE TERRITORY, I'LL BE HELPING YOU!

OKAY! LEAD THE WAY!
SPIN SPIN SPIN!
RUN RUN RUN!

STOP!
??

WHY'D YOU STOP? ARE WE THERE ALREADY?
NO. I DIDN'T SAY I WAS GOING **WITH** YOU. I ONLY SAID I WAS **GUIDING** YOU.

PEACH TREE
THIS IS THE BEST I CAN DO FOR YOU.
HEAD TO THE PEACH TREE!
No way.

C'MON, I THOUGHT YOU WERE THE BEST? YOU'RE ALEADY GIVING UP? *TYPICAL HUMAN.*
JUNG? WHERE'D YOU COME FROM?

TCH!
And... SHUT UP!

NOW, LET'S SEE ABOUT THIS...

HMM. IF I...
Point

Resultant Vector
A°
Second Vector
B°
C°
First Vector

UGH!

WIN!
Yeah!

ROUTE PLANNED.

WATCH ME!
HOW DID I GET HERE?
WHOOSH!

CHAPTER 7

ZOOOM!
I'LL TAKE THAT!
GRAB!

THIS IS CRAZY!
RAMP!

. . .

WOW.

THIS IS AWESOME!

AHH!
WAIT!
NOPE!
I WAS ENTIRELY RIGHT THE FIRST TIME!
THIS IS CRAZY!
THUMP
THUMP.
THUMP!

WHOA!
AHH!
SKID OUT!
JUMP!
HAH!
LAND!
JUMP!
JUMP!
JUMP!

AND NOW FOR THE HARD PART!

HEY UGLY!
GRUH?
ISLAND MONSTER (NOTABLY UGLY)

WHAMM!
DODGE!
HAH! TOO SLOW!

C'MON, GRETA! IT'S OUR CHANCE!
WHUMP.

OKAY LEGS, DO YOUR MAGIC!
UPHILL CLIMB!
SEE YA, SUCKER!
ZOOM!
HARVEY (SUCKER)
LEAP!

BUH!
LAUNCH!

GRAB!
SOAR!
AAAND... NOW!
FLOAT!
FLOAT! FLOAT!
SQUEEZE!
DON'T WORRY, GRETA! I'VE GOT YOU!

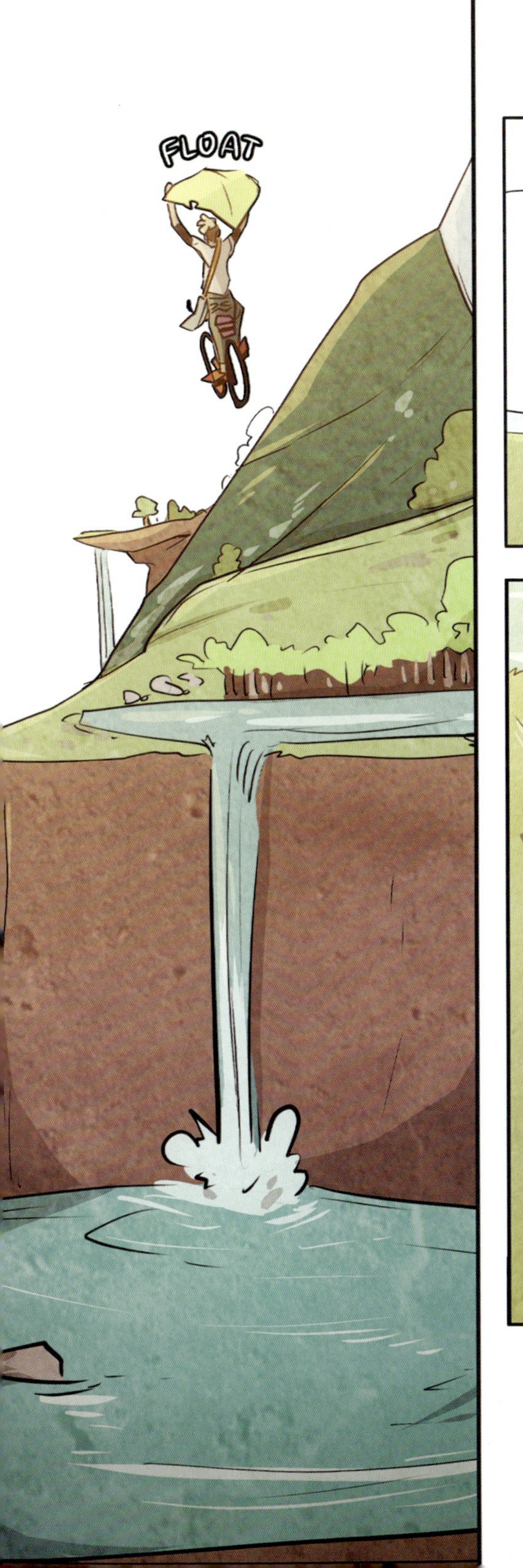
FLOAT

THUMP!

OUCH!

HAH! I GOT THE PACKAGE!

ALTHOUGH... WHAT DO I DO WITH IT NOW?

HELLO, TALL PIG!
GAHH!
DON'T CALL ME THAT!
OKAY, OKAY.
NOW, YOU NEED TO TAKE THE PACKAGE TO 113 PEBBLELANE.
BUT DON'T WORRY, THE HARD PART IS DONE.

IT'S ALL DOWNHILL FROM HERE.
THAT'S NOT DOWNHILL!
THAT'S **DOWNCLIFF!**
WELL, I GUESS YOU COULD QUIT.

~SIGH~
C'MON, GRETA.

THREE HOURS LATER.
WALK
WALK
STUMBLE
WALK

TRUDGE TRUDGE TRUDGE

HEY, SMIRKLEY. I'M HOME. DID YOU MISS ME?

DID YOU MISS MY COMFORTING PRESENCE, OR THE ADORABLE WAY I PUT FOOD IN YOUR BOWL?
meowrr
MLEM!
HOW DID I GET HERE?

PAT
TAKE A NAP, GRETA. YOU DID **GREAT** TODAY.

SO DID I.
HOW DID I GET HERE?

Ha ha ha ha ha ha ha ha ha!

CHAPTER 8

YOU MISSED MY PARTY YESTERDAY!
LIKE, ALL OF IT!
EXCEPT FOR THAT WEIRD PART WHERE YOU CAME IN, ACTED WEIRD FOR TWO MINUTES, THEN WEIRDLY LEFT.
SORRY, I HAD TO GO INTO WORK.
I THOUGHT DYNASTY QUIT DELIVERING AFTER SIX?
TEA FOR YOU!
RADIO
THEY DO.
I MEANT THE NEW JOB.

OH YEAH, WHAT ARE YOU DOING AGAIN?
JUST MORE DELIVERIES. NOTHING STRANGE ABOUT IT.

I DIDN'T SAY IT WAS STRANGE. BUT NOW I'M SUSPICIOUS.
I'M LIKE, NATURALLY SUSPICIOUS AND UNNATURALLY SUSPICIOUS, BOTH.

ARE YOU DOING SOMETHING ILLEGAL? IS IT **FUN ILLEGAL**?

I TOLD YOU, JUST MORE DELIVERIES.
YEAH, WELL, I TOTALLY DELIVERED A CUTE GUY TO YOU LAST NIGHT. AND YOU DECIDED TO GO AND STAMP HIM AS...

RETURN TO SENDER

RETURN TO SENDER
REJECTED

SORRY! BUT I'M NOT EVEN SURE I'M LOOOKING TO DATE ANYONE RIGHT NOW.
WRONG ATTITUDE, DARE! GET BACK INTO THE DATING POOL OR ELSE YOU'RE GOING TO END UP MARRYING SMIRKLEY.
AND THEN YOU'LL GET EVEN MORE CATS!
STRETCH!

YOU'LL END UP LIKE ONE OF
THOSE POLYAMOROUS CAT BRIDES

KNOCK!
KNOCK!

HERE THAT?
IT'S PROBABLY THE PREACHER, COME TO PRONOUNCE YOU CAT AND WIFE.
I'M BETTING IT'S SOMEONE FROM THE INSANE ASYLUM, COME TO TAKE YOU AWAY.

GOOD.
I COULD USE THE FREE RENT.
SPEAKING OF FREE STUFF, I'M NABBING MORE OF THESE DELICIOUS COOKIES. I BET TOM WOULD LOVE THEM.
OR MOTORPOOL.
SHE'S TOTALLY CRAZY! THE TWO OF YOU WOULD GET ALONG PERFECTLY!
KNOCK!
KNOCK!
MOTORPOOL'S THAT GIRL AGAIN, RIGHT? SOMEONE'S SISTER?

OPEN!

HEY, TALL PIG! HOW'S IT GOING?
707
W-W-WHAT ARE YOU DOING HERE?!
I BROUGHT YOUR PAY FOR THE COMPLETED MISSION!
TROT TROT TROT
LET'S SEE, WHAT'S BEST FOR STEALING COOKIES?
PLASTIC BAG?
PAPER BAG?
ZIPBOY
LULU'S HERE, YOU IDIOT!
SHE'LL SEE YOU!
707
OOH...
AND QUIT CALLING ME TALL PIG!
SURE, SURE I'LL MAKE IT QUICK.
HERE'S YOUR GOLD.
BINK!
GOLD
24K
GOLD BARS:
ESTIMATED WORTH... FOUR THOUSAND DOLLARS.

DARE? YOU HAVE ANY TUPPERWARE I CAN BORROW?

CUPBOARD TO THE RIGHT OF THE SINK!
HIDE THE GOLD.
HIDE THE GOLD
HIDE THE GOLD.

THE BRIDE OF BIG MAN KARLON
THERE!
HIDDEN!
GOLD!

BINK!
KNICKS + KNACKS!
GRAB & GO!
PUSH!
I BROUGHT THIS, TOO.
HOLY CRAP!!!

DARE, YOU OKAY?
I JUST STUBBED MY TOE.

KNICKS + KNACKS!
GRAB & GO!
PUSH!
I AM GOING TO KICK YOU SO HARD IF YOU DON'T GET RID OF THAT THING!

YOU'LL GET ME IN TROUBLE WITH LULU!
SHE CAN'T KNOW ABOUT ANY OF THIS!

CALM DOWN, TALL PIG. YOU CAN JUST HIDE IT IN A POCKET UNIVERSE.
WHAT?!
BINK!

YOU CAN ACCESS IT WHENEVER YOU WANT, VIA THIS KEY!
ptink!

WHY DO I NEED TO ACCESS IT? WHAT WAS THAT THING?

...WHAT MAGIC DO YOU WANT?

CHAPTER 9

THE DISPENSARY:
A.K.A. THE VENDING MACHINE
FOR MAGICAL BIKE PARTS.
DARE CRILLEY:
CURRENTLY NERVOUS
BICYCLE MESSENGER.

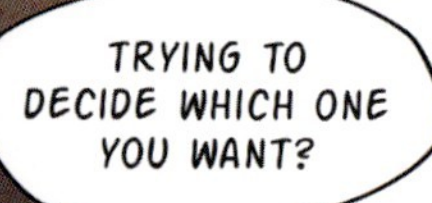
TRYING TO
DECIDE WHICH ONE
YOU WANT?

YEP.
PIBBS: GOD GUIDE.
DIVINE IN NATURE, THOUGH NOT
NECESSARILY IN CHARACTER.

SCARED
OF CHOOSING?
YEP.
PUSH

DARE! **SERIOUSLY!**
YOU HAVE A CROW IN
YOUR KITCHEN!
LULU DEL CARMEN:
DARE'S BEST FRIEND.
CROW: ???

HMM.
SCUTTLE!

WHAT ARE YOU?
A NEW ROOMMATE?
YOU PAYING RENT?
GOT A JOB OR
SOMETHING?
I SUPPOSE WINGS ARE
GOOD FOR DELIVERING
YOU COULD BE LIKE,
DARE'S SIDEKICK.

TAP TAP TAP
HOW CAN I TELL WHAT THESE ACTUALLY DO?

PUSH!
THERE IS AN INSTRUCTION PAMPHLET.
BINK!
Ooo! It's MAGIC!

THAT'S NOT A PAMPHLET, THAT'S A MONUMENT!
THERE'S ONLY LIKE TWENTY THINGS TO CHOOSE FROM. WHY IS IT SO BIG?
Ooo! It's MAGIC!
THUMP!

KNICKS + KNACKS!
THESE ARE ONLY THE ITEMS SHOWING RIGHT NOW.
THERE ARE ACTUALLY FIFTY-SIX THOUSAND, THREE HUNDRED AND TWELVE ITEMS.

FIFTY-SIX THOUSAND, THREE HUNDRED AND TWELVE?

KNICKS + KNACKS!
I'LL BE RIGHT BACK.
PUSH
RADIO

OH, HEY DARE!
THERE YOU ARE.
SO, WE'VE GOT A LITTLE BIT OF A **"CROW IN THE KITCHEN"** SITUATION GONG ON HERE.
UHH... DARE? HELLO?
WOW. THAT'S A LOT.
GLUG GLUG GLUG
SO... ABOUT THAT CROW. WHICH IS ON THE COUNTER NEXT TO YOU.
GLUG GLUG GLUG
SLUTTLE!
COOL.
I'LL JUST STAND HERE.
BEING IGNORED.
WITH THE CROW.
GLUG GLUG GLUG!
GOOD TALK, DARE. I HAD FUN CHATTING.

OKAY. WE SHOULD START READING AT PAGE ONE.
THERE'S SOME WARNINGS YOU SHOULD BE AWARE-
STRIDE!
STRIDE
STRIDE
STRIDE
NUDGE!
Ooo! It's MAGIC!

POKE POKE
RANDOM
POKE!
OF?
Ooo! It's MAGIC!

DID YOU JUST... CHOOSE AT RANDOM?
YES.

THERE'S NO WAY I'M GOING TO LEARN EVERYTHING IN THIS MANUAL. I'M NOT A BOOK LEARNER
SO I MADE A REASONABLE DECISION TO PANIC AND JUST HIT A BUTTON.
NUDGE
NUDGE
Ooo! It's MAGIC!

FAIR ENOUGH. PART OF WHY WE CHOSE YOU IS BECAUSE YOU TAKE DECISIVE ACTONS.
YOU DON'T WANT TO BE RIDING ACROSS A SPLINK HILL AND HAVE A FODDLERANGLE TWIST ITS LOG YOUNG AT YOUR BIKE, AND THEN WASTE YOUR TIME WONDERING IF YOU SHOULD DIG A CRANIAL PIT OR SPRAY THE LIME WADDLE.

TUP TUP THUMP!
WHAT THE HELL ARE YOU TALKING ABOUT?
ARE THOSE EVEN WORDS!?

ELSEWHERE...

ADMINISTRATIVE OFFICES
BILTON TROLLEY:
GODDESS OF OPTIMISM
SO, TORGA, YOU'RE SAYING JUNG FINALLY HIRED A MESSENGER?

THAT'S GREAT!
SIMPLY FANTASTIC!
COULDN'T BE BETTER NEWS!

I TAKE IT JUNG'S RESOLVED HIS ISSUES WITH HUMANS THEN?
OH, NO MA'AM. NOT AT ALL.
HE'S GOING TO BE A CONSTANT THREAT TO DARE CRILLEY. SHE'LL HAVE TO AVOID HIM AT ALL COSTS.

HE'LL LIKELY UNDERMINE EVERYTHING SHE TRIES TO DO, MAKING ANY DELIVERY TEN TIMES AS DANGEROUS, HOPING THAT SHE'LL FAIL, ULTIMATELY DOOMING US ALL BECAUSE OF HIS UNRESOLVED MENTAL TRAUMA.

FANTASTIC! THAT'S WHAT I WANT TO HEAR! WE SHOULD CELEBRATE!
AND I HEAR SHE'S ALREADY COMPLETED A DELIVERY? EXCELLENT! SO EXCELLENT!

THAT'S ONE DELIVERY DOWN...

...ONLY A FEW MORE TO GO!

MEANWHILE...

LET'S CLIP IT ONTO YOUR BIKE...

CHAPTER 10

MYSTERIOUS MAGICAL ITEM.
CLIP!

SO... ANY ADVICE ON HOW TO ACTIVATE THIS THING AND FIND OUT WHAT IT DOES?
JUST RIDE AROUND, I SUPPOSE.

SNIFF SNIFF SNORT
IT'LL BE APPARENT RIGHT AWAY IF IT HELPS YOU GO FASTER OR FLY.

IF IT LETS YOU CHANGE SIZE, OR SUMMON TURTLES, YOU MIGHT NEVER ACTIVATE IT BY CHANCE.
IT'S TRUE THAT I'M RARELY TRYING TO SUMMON TURTLES.

I SUPPOSE IT'S NOT SAFE TO RIDE GRETA AROUND THE CITY RIGHT NOW. WOULD YOU MIND IF I GOT A TRIP TO FELDANA?
PEDAL PEDAL RIDE RIDE

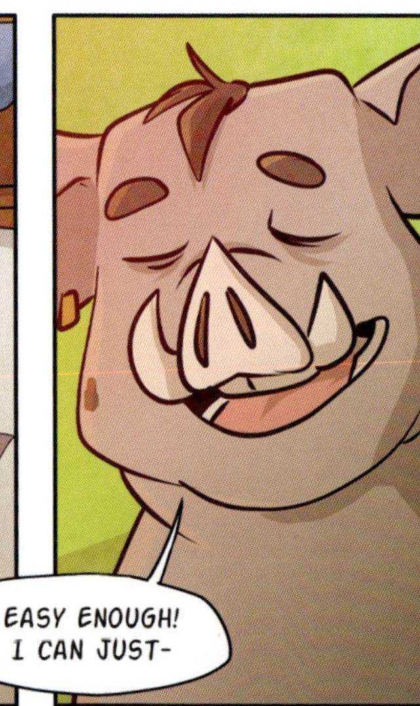
EASY ENOUGH! I CAN JUST-

?
A PORTAL! THANKS!

DARE, JUST A MINUTE. I...
PEDAL PEDAL RIDE RIDE!

...DIDN'T MAKE THAT PORTAL.
VEEOOP!

HMM.

?
hop hop bop

COME HERE, MR. CROW. IF YOU'RE GOING TO-
HUH?

DARE! NOW THERE'S A PIG HERE, TOO!

DO YOU KNOW THAT THEY CONSIDER THE INVENTION OF FIRE TO BE THEIR FIRST STEP TOWARDS CIVILIZATION?

JUNG, I UNDERSTAND THAT-
NO! LISTEN TO ME!
I'LL NEVER FORGET THE LOOK ON MARADA'S FACE WHEN SHE REALIZED SHE WOULDN'T MAKE IT OUT OF THE FIRE.

AND THAT THERE WAS NOTHING I COULD DO.
THERE WAS NOW WAY I COULD SAVE HERE.

YOU CAN TELL ME THAT DARE WASN'T THERE WHEN MARADA DIED. THAT SHE WASN'T TO BLAME. YOU CAN EVEN TELL ME NO HUMAN ALIVE WAS THERE.

AND I'LL AGREE WITH YOU UNTIL THE END OF TIME.
BUT WHEN I LOOK AT ANY HUMAN, I DON'T SEE THEIR EYES OR THEIR SMILES.
I SEE MARADA'S FACE WHEN SHE REALIZED SHE WOULDN'T MAKE IT OUT OF THE FIRE.

BACK TO...
KNOCK! KNOCK! KNOCK!

MOTORPOOL?
THANK GOD!

FOLLOW ME!
STRIDE STRIDE STRIDE

HUH!?

OKAY, LULU, I HAVE TO ADMIT...
...WHEN YOU CALLED AND SAID YOU WERE HERE...

...THAT YOUR FRIEND MYSTERIOUSLY VANISHED...
...AND THERE WAS A CROW AND A PIG WITH YOU...

...I HONESTLY THOUGHT YOU WERE TOTALLY DRUNK, HIGH, OR ABSOLUTELY CRAZY.

BUT THIS HERE IS A PIG...
...AND THAT'S DEFINITELY A CROW.

I'M FULLY AWARE OF THAT, AND I'M FULLY FREAKING OUT.
WHAT DO WE DO?
NOT SURE. WHY'D YOU CALL **ME?**
THIS IS ALL CRAZY, AND YOU'RE THE CRAZIEST PERSON I KNOW.
PLUS YOU HAVE THIS PIG TATTOO.
POINK!
DUDE, I'VE GOT A LOT OF TATTOOS.
THIS ONE'S AN OCTOPUS IN A THREESOME. DOESN'T MEAN I'M AN EXPERT ON THE SUBJECT.
SO, WHAT SHOULD WE DO?
I'M THINKING...
...WE CALL SOME OTHER PEOPLE AND GET DRUNK?

OKAY. LET'S DO IT.

?
WHOOOOSH
AHHH HHHHH!
HELLO?!

??
AHHHH HHHHH!!
WHOOOOOOSH!

???
AHHHHH HHHHH!!!
WHOOOOOOSH

HEY, DID YOU JUST HEAR A SCREAM?

CHAPTER 11

VOOOP!
AHHH!

THUMP!
UGH.

UHH...

GOONG!
GAHH!

HELLO!
AAHH!

I'M BENTS, THE GOD OF AWKWARD COMPLIMENTS.
AND YOU MUST BE... DARE?
UH, YEAH?

RIGHT. GOOD.
AMAZING THAT A MERE HUMAN MADE IT INTO THESE CAVES!
AND YET HERE YOU ARE, DESPITE ALL YOUR DEFICIENCIES!
BRAVO!

I'M NOT EMBARRASSED TO BE HUMAN.
GOOD FOR YOU! HOW BRAVE!
NOW, THIS NEEDS TO BE DELIVERED TO...

...EDMUND HYACINTH, THE GOD
F UNPUBLISHED ROMANCE NOVELS
THE TEMPEST OF THE NIGHT CARESSED IM LIKE THE KNOWING HANDS OF A RAGING ARABIAN PRINCE!
"OH NIGHT!" HE CRIED. "OH PRINCE!"
OUTSIDE, THE CAMELS MOOED IN THEIR PENS.

OOF. THAT WAS TERRIBLE.
YEAH, HE'S REALLY BAD.
ANYWAY, YOU HAVE FIFTEEN MINUTES...

...BEFORE IT'S
WAR BETWEEN THE GODS

DIRECTIONS ARE IN THAT SEALED LETTER.
HAVE FUN!
RADIO

RADIO
WAIT! I-

BLINK
RADIO
LOOK!
~MOAN~

COUNTDOWN

15:00

COUNTDOWN: 14:52

WHY NOT? DARE'S AWESOME AND SHE HAS LEGS THAT ARE LIKE ***BOOM BOOM P-KOW***

COUNTDOWN: 12:06
PEDAL PEDAL
CHURN CHURN
ALMOST ACROSS SCRIMSHAW MEADOW! I CAN DO THIS!

COUNTDOWN: 11:55
AND NOW I JUST NEED TO GO AROUND...

COUNTDOWN: 11:53
...THIS LAKE?
YOU'RE KIDDING ME! IT'S HUGE!

UHM... EXCUSE ME? HOW FAR AROUND IS THIS LAKE?
AROUND THE LAKE?
COUNTDOWN: 11:50

COUNTDOWN: 11:33
WELL... IT GOES **INFINITE** IN THAT DIRECTION.
AND A BIT FARTHER THAT WAY.
RADIO

WAR!
DESTRUCTION!
END OF THE WORLD!
ALL DARE'S FAULT!
COUNTDOWN: 11:27
TICK TICK TICK
!
I MIGHT BE IN TROUBLE HERE.
RADIO

CHAPTER 12

COUNTDOWN: 11:26
OKAY, SO I HAVE ELEVEN MINUTES TO RACE AROUND AN INFINITE LAKE.
RADIO
COUNTDOWN: 11:21
PROBABLY IMPOSSIBLE, BUT I'M GOING TO GO OUT TRYING.
YOU CAN SAY THAT **DARE SALT CRILLEY** TRIED AND FAILED,
INFINITE
BUT YOU CAN NEVER SAY THAT I FAILED TO TRY.

COUNTDOWN: 11:16

GRETA! YOU AND I ARE GOING TO STICK CLOSE TO THE SHORE!
EVERY INCH COUNTS!
PEDAL PEDAL PEDAL
OR... MAYBE IT DOESN'T? INFINITE IS HARD.

COUNTDOWN: 11:09
AND WHAT WAS WITH ALL THOSE PORTALS, ANYWAY?
HOW DID I END UP BACK IN FELDANA?
RADIO

COUNTDOWN: 11:05
DID PIBBS..?
WHOOSH
WHOOSH

COUNTDOWN: 11:04
UHH...
RADIO

COUNTDOWN: 11:03
SLOSH!
EEEEEERT!

COUNTDOWN: 11:01
WHAT IN THE-

COUNTDOWN: 10:59
HMM.

COUNTDOWN: 10:57
LET ME JUST-

COUNTDOWN: 10:55
SPLASH!
RADIO
AHHH!

COUNTDOWN: 10:50
HAHA! I CAN RIDE ON FREAKIN' WATER! MY NEW BIKE PART IS AWESOME!
RADIO

COUNTDOWN: 10:35
BEWARE, OTHER SIDE OF THE SHORE...
...I'M COMING FOR YOU!
COUNTDOWN: 10:04
SLOSH
SLOSH
SLOSH
COUNTDOWN: 8:27
SLOSH SLOSH WHOOSH!

COUNTDOWN: 7:04
SLOSH
SLOSH SLOSH!

MEANWHILE...
I HAVE A PIG ON A LEASH AND IT MAKES ME FEEL LIKE A ROCK STAR, OR AN ECCENTRIC BILLIONAIRE.
I WANT TO RIDE THE PIG.

YOU THINK HE'D BE OKAY WITH THAT? MAYBE HE'D BUCK ME OFF?
DO PIGS EVEN BUCK? AND BY THE WAY, WHERE ARE WE GOING?

MY EX-BOYFRIEND'S. HE OWNS A BAR WITH A BACKYARD.

HE KEEPS WANTING TO OPEN A BEER GARDEN,
BUT THERE'S ACCESSIBILITY LAWS SO HE'S WAITING FOR PERMITS.

I CAN TAKE CARE OF THE PIG THERE WHILE YOU FIND DARE.
I MEAN, HER BIKE WAS GONE. I'M NOT ALL THAT WORRIED.

IT WAS PROBABLY SOME DELIVERY THAT NEEDED TO BE DONE RIGHT AWAY,
I'LL FIND HER. I JUST WISH SHE'D ANSWER HER PHONE.

I'LL LET YOU KNOW HOW IT TURNS OUT WITH THE PIG.
OKAY! BYE, MOTORPOOL! BYE, PIG!

BYE, LULU!

DID THAT PIG JUST TALK?

MEANWHILE IN FELDANA...
SUNTAN LOTION
ANTI-CUPID LOTION
COUNTDOWN: 2:48
HA HA HA HA!
THE SHORE!
WHOOOOSH!
COUNTDOWN: 2:29
I AM DARE CRILLEY!
COUNTDOWN: 1:04
OKAY, SO I NEED TO FIND CABIN THREE.
ONE, TWO, AND...
COUNTDOWN: 1:36
...THREE!
SKRRT!
COUNTDOWN: 1:32
HUH?
THPP!

OUNTDOWN: 1:19
Hello!
Edmund Hyacinth, here!
I had to step out.
I'm currently visiting
with friends in
Cabin One. If you
need me, just
go there and knock!
♡EH
COUNTDOWN: 1:12
BUT...BUT... ...THE DELIVERY NOTICE SAID TO **NEVER** KNOCK ON THE OTHER CABIN DOORS.

COUNTDOWN: 0:59
WELL... HERE'S CABIN NUMBER ONE.
RADIO
TRUDGE
TRUDGE
FLAP
FLAP
COUNTDOWN: 0:48
RADIO
TREMBLE
TREMBLE

COUNTDOWN: 0:41
TREMBLE
TREMBLE

HA HA
HA
HA!
COUNTDOWN: 0:32

RADIO

CHAPTER 13

COUNTDOWN: 0:29
HA HA HA HA HA!
HEY, WAIT A MINUTE...

COUNTDOWN: 0:27
RADIO
JUNG!? IS THAT YOU?
I'D KNOW YOUR MOCKING LAUGH ANYWHERE.

HA HA HA! WHAT ARE YOU GOING TO DO, HUMAN?
YOU CAN'T KNOCK ON THE DOOR!
I SPECIFICALLY HAD THAT ADDED TO THE REQUEST.

COUNTDOWN: 0:25
AND NOW YOU'RE GOING TO FAIL.
LIKE ALL HUMANS DO.

BECAUSE DARE CRILLEY IS NO BETTER THAN-

COUNTDOWN: 0:17

SLIDE
HELLO? WHAT'S ALL THIS NOISE?
SOME DUMB CROW FLEW INTO THE DOOR.
WEIRD, RIGHT?
ANYWAY, EDMUND HYACINTH? LETTER FOR YOU.

FOR ME? OH, BOUNTY OF JOY!
THE TREMBLE OF MY BREAST IS AN ERUPTING GEYSER OF DELIGHT!

COUNTDOWN: 0:11

RADIO
YEP. WHATEVER.
THE IMPORTANT THING IS...

...DELIVERY **COMPLETED**, YOU BIG BALL OF JERK FEATHERS.

ELSEWHERE...

BARTENDER, BRING ME ANOTHER.

SUSHI CABOOSE
I'M NOT A BARTENDER, LULU. I'M A SUSHI CHEF.
YOU'RE AT **SUSHI CABOOSE**, REMEMBER?
TED
THEN BRING ME SOME FISH LEGS AND ALSO A BARTENDER.

UH HUH. EXCEPT, NO.
YOU OKAY TODAY, SIS?
TED
YOU SEEM A LITTLE... HOW CAN I PUT THIS? **SUPER WEIRD.**

I HEARD A PIG TALK TODAY.
WELL, THAT'S NO BIG THING. HOW MANY DRINKS DID YOU HAVE FIRST?

SUSHI CABOOSE
MANY DRINKS. BUT I WAS SOBER WHEN I HEARD THE PIG TALK.
TED
OH, THEN I GUESS IT IS A BIG THING. HOW LONG HAVE YOU BEEN HAVING HALLUCINATIONS?

WHAT HAPPENED TO MY SUPPORTIVE BROTHER?
THE ONE WHO ALWAYS BELIEVED ME WHENEVER I SAID ANYTHING STRANGE?

WONDER WHO THAT GUY WAS?
BECAUSE I'M PRETTY SURE I'M A TOTAL JERK.
TED

HEY BOSS? AM I A TOTAL JERK?
TED
BOSS
DON'T INVOLVE ME IN YOUR FAMILY DRAMA, TED.

SEE? IF I WASN'T A JERK, SHE'D RESPECT ME MORE.
I AGREE THAT THE EVIDENCE IS SUBSTANTIAL.
TED

MAYBE YOU'RE JUST LONELY.
GOT A SPECIAL SOMEONE?
IF YOU HAD SOMEONE TO TALK TO, MAYBE YOU WOULDN'T THINK PIGS WERE TALKING.

NOPE, NO
ONE FOR ME.
AND WHY DO PEOPLE ALWAYS THINK THAT'S SO IMPORTANT?
PUSH!
I CAN STAND ON MY OWN TWO FEET, YOU KNOW.

SWIPE!
YOU'RE SITTING ON YOUR OWN TWO BUTT CHEEKS RIGHT NOW, BUT I ACCEPT YOUR ANSWER.
SO HOW'VE YOU BEEN SPENDING YOUR TIME LATELY, MRS. SINGLE LADY?

IT'S *MISS* SINGLE LADY, THAN YOU VERY MUCH.
AND I'VE BEEN TRYING TO SET DARE UP ON SOME DATES.
SHE'S A TOTAL WRECK AND NEEDS SOMEONE TO COMPLETE HER.

UH HUH. HEY, BOSS? ARE YOU HEARING THIS HYPOCRISY?
TED
BOSS
FAMILY DRAMA, TED.

RING
RING
RING
CALL INCOMING
DARE!
ANSWER

RING! RING!
AH! IT'S DARE!!

HEY! WHERE ARE YOU? I'VE BEEN WORRIED SICK!
SORRY, LULU!

HAD AN EMERGENCY DELIVERY. THINGS GOT... COMPLICATED.
BUT YOU'RE OKAY?

ME? SURE. I'M TOTALLY FINE.
NOBODY'S HURT.

PAD
PAD
PAD

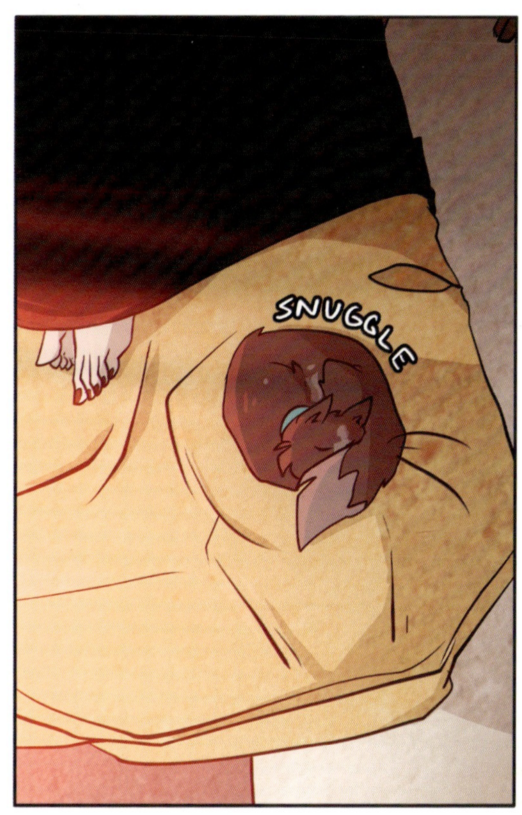
SNUGGLE

AT LEAST NO HUMANS WERE HURT, ANYWAY.
9:23

CHAPTER 14

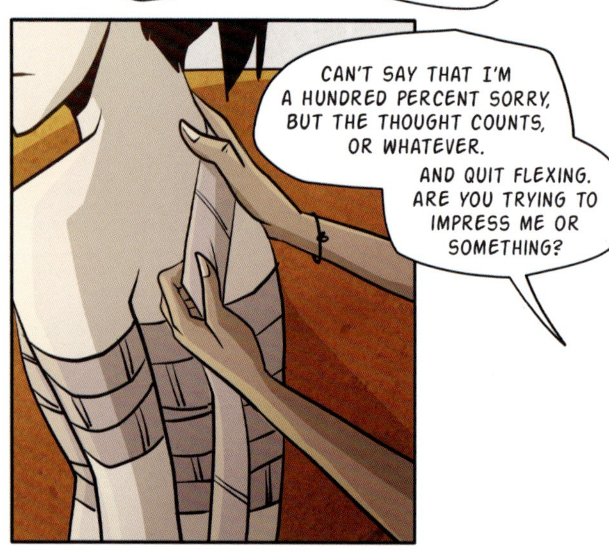

I'VE SEEN PLENTY OF NAKED GUYS BEFORE AND YOU'RE NOT EXACTLY THE PICK OF THE LITTER, CROW BOY.

REALLY? AND HOW MANY OF THOSE NAKED MEN WERE **GODS**?

OH GEEZ. MAYBE...THREE OF THEM?
GODS IN BED, ANYWAY.
Sigh...

SO WHERE DID YOU GET THESE BANDAGES? THEY DON'T FEEL NORMAL.
THEY'RE CAFÉ NAPKINS.

HUH, THAT'S NOT WEIRD AT ALL.
IF YOU REMEMBER, I'M THE GOD OF CAFÉ NAPKINS.

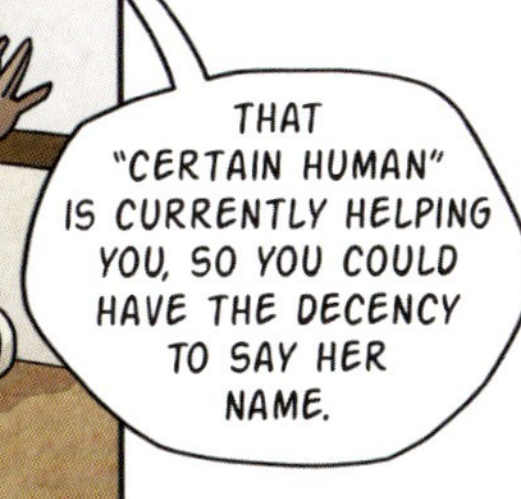
THESE WILL BIND TO ME AND HEAL THE DAMAGE CAUSED BY A CERTAIN **HUMAN** WHEN SHE HURLED ME INTO A DOOR.
THAT "CERTAIN HUMAN" IS CURRENTLY HELPING YOU, SO YOU COULD HAVE THE DECENCY TO SAY HER NAME.

BURNN

PAP
PAP
PAP

HAH!
SETTLE
AT LEAST YOUR CAT REGARDS ME WITH RESPECT.

FALSE PREMISE. MR. SMIRKLEY ONLY SITS ON PEOPLE BECAUSE HE LIKES TO FART ON THEM.
GHOST

PFFT!
IT'S HIS THING.

CURSES!

AWAY FROM ME, **FOUL BEAST!** OR ELSE I'LL-!
RRR!

GET CLOCKED WITH A BIKE LOCK IF YOU EVEN COME CLOSE TO THREATENING MY CAT!

NOW SIT DOWN.
I'M GOING TO FINISH YOUR BANDAGES, KICK YOU OUT OF MY APARTMENT, AND THEN HOPEFULLY I WON'T EVER SEE YOU AGAIN.

IT'S NO WONDER ALL THE GODS ARE A MESS IF THEY'RE LIKE YOU.
YOU'RE THE GOD OF CRY-BABIES.
THE GOD OF SELF-IMPORTANT STICKS UP THE BUTT.

NOW HOLD THIS ICE PACK IN PLACE.
ARE YOU A BIG ENOUGH BOY TO DO THAT?
DO NOT TALK TO ME IN THAT MANNER.

MY POINT IS THAT I'M TRYING NOT TO TALK TO YOU AT ALL.
NOW JUST STAY THERE A BIT.

POINK!
I NEED TO CHOOSE ANOTHER MAGIC ITEM.

HMMM...

CHOOSE 187AG9.
WHY?

IT'S A MAGIC PORTAL CREATOR.
YOU'LL BE ABLE TO GO BACK AND FORTH BETWEEN THIS WORLD AND FELDANA ON YOUR OWN.
PAD PAD PAD

OH. THANKS.
BEEP BEEP BOP

I ONLY TOLD YOU SO YOU'D QUIT BOTHERING MY FRIENDS.
BUT THEY'RE EAGER ENOUGH TO HELP. THEY SEEM TO THINK YOU'RE AMUSING.

THE ONLY THING THAT'S AMUSING IS THAT THEY PUT UP WITH YOU.
TORGA IS THE KINDEST GIANT GOD I'VE MET SO FAR...
...AND EVEN THOUGH PIBBS IS INFURIATING, HE'S NOT TRYING TO SABOTAGE ME ALL THE TIME.
WHAT HAVE YOU GOT AGAINST ME, ANYWAY?
YOUR FOUL HUMANITY! IT'S A DISEASE!
YOUR KIND ARE NOTHING BUT TROUBLE AND DESTRUCTION! BOMBS WAITING TO EXPLODE!

SAYS THE SO-CALLED "SUPERIOR BEING" WHO'S SO PETTY HE'S WILLING TO RISK THE **DESTRUCTION OF THE ENTIRE UNIVERSE** JUST TO MAKE ME LOOK BAD.

SO, IN YOUR FACE, CROW BOY.
NOW TAKE YOUR SMUG SMILE AND GET OUT OF MY APARTMENT!

GRRRR

GRRRRR

UM, HELLO?

!
SORRY TO BUTT IN, BUT THE DOOR WAS OPEN AND...

...WHO'S THE SHIRTLESS GUY THAT SMELLS LIKE FRESHLY MADE PANCAKES?

CHAPTER 15

FOOP!

BUTTON
BUTTON

STRUT
STRUT
LEAVE

SLAMM!!

TREMBLE
WHAT'S HIS NAME?
WHY DOES HE SMELL LIKE PANCAKES?
IS THIS THE REAL REASON WHY YOU VANISHED?
OH DEAR HEAVEN. DID YOU GET **LAID?**
CLAP CLAP
CAN YOU BELIEVE THOSE EYES?
HOW DID HE GET INJURED?
SHAKE! SHAKE! SHAKE!
OH MY GOD DID YOU SLEEP WITH HIM **SO HARD** THAT YOU BROKE HIM?
ICK! GROSS! I WOULD NEVER SLEEP WITH JUNG.
HE'S SO... **NOT** SLEEPABLE WITH.
BLEH!
BTS
IN FACT I'M NOT EVEN SURE IT WOULD BE LEGAL, FROM A COSMIC SENSE.
HUH?

NEVER MIND. AND JUNG'S JUST ONE OF THE BOSSES AT MY NEW JOB.
AT LEAST HE THINKS HE IS.

SPEAKING OF, I HAVE TO GO TO MY REGULAR JOB NOW!
PHSSS!
I'M SO SORRY! I KNOW WE HAVE A LOT TO TALK ABOUT!
SMELL B GONE
ANTIPERSPIRANT
ANTI-WANTING-TO-TALK-ABOUT-JUNG

C'MON GRETA!
WE RIDE!

NO! DARE! WAIT!
RIDE!

SLAMM!
CLOCK C

SLUMP!
DANG IT. I WANTED TO TELL HER ABOUT TALKING PIGS.

PAP PAP PAP

SETTLE!

FART!
BTS

BLAUGHDO'S BAKERY
WHOOSH!

OH DANG! I'M GOING TO BE LATE!
I NEED TO... TO...HMM...

BRAAAKE!

GRETA! I HAVE A **FANTASTIC** IDEA!
FIRST, I'M PUTTING THIS MAGIC STICKER ON YOU.

I'LL USE THE STICKER TO MAKE A PORTAL TO FELDANA, THEN MAKE A SECOND PORTAL THERE THAT OPENS RIGHT IN FRONT OF WORK!
IT'LL BE LIKE TELEPORTING!
STICK!

LET'S GET A BIT OF PRIVACY, AND...
WASTE

POKE!

NICE!
I'M A GENIUS!
VLOOP!

WE RIDE!

THWOOP!
OOPS! WHOA! YIKES!
UH, HELLO!

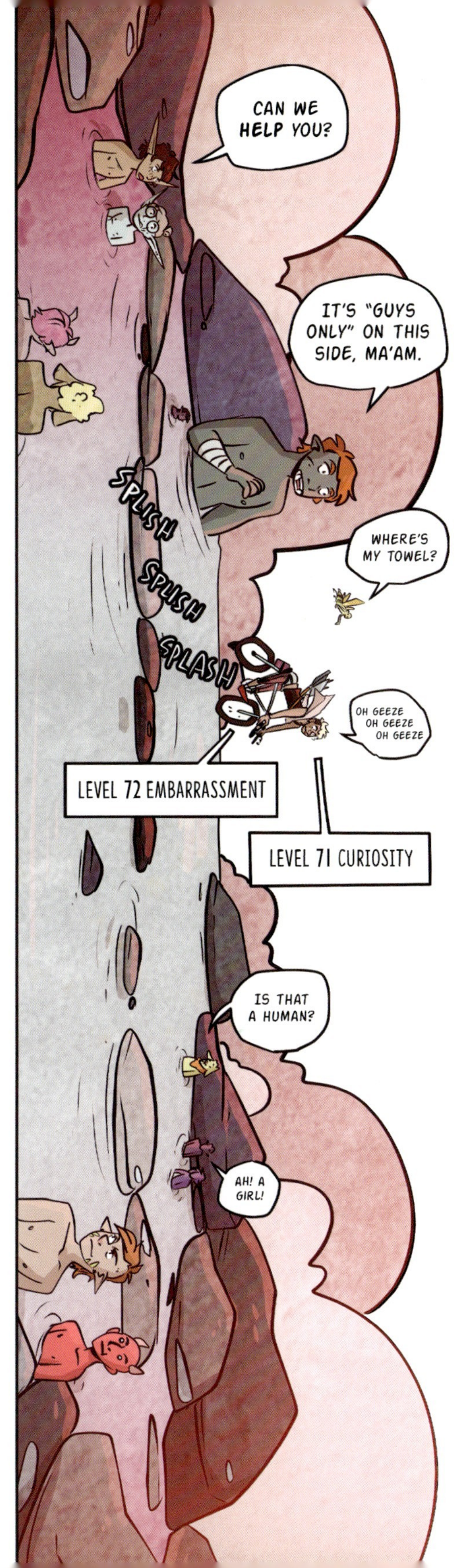
CAN WE HELP YOU?
IT'S "GUYS ONLY" ON THIS SIDE, MA'AM.
WHERE'S MY TOWEL?
SPLISH
SPLISH
SPLASH
OH GEEZE OH GEEZE OH GEEZE
LEVEL 72 EMBARRASSMENT
LEVEL 71 CURIOSITY
IS THAT A HUMAN?
AH! A GIRL!

PORTAL! PORTAL! PORTAL! PORTAL!
POKE! POKE! POKE! POKE!
AH, THERE!
RIDE! FLEE! ESCAPE!

WHUMPFFF!

HAH! RIGHT OUTSIDE WORK!
EVERYTHING WORKED OUT PERFECTLY!
DYNASY
Dynasty Delivery Service

UH-OH. WHERE'D I GET THIS TOWEL?

WAS THAT THE HUMAN?
I BELIEVE IT WAS.
WHAT AN ADORABLE LITTLE SPECIES THEY ARE!
DO THEY ALL LOOK LIKE THAT?

I THINK NOT. BUT I WAS MORE INTRIGUED BY SOMETHING ELSE.
I COULDN'T LOOK MYSELF IN THE MIRROR AND TAKE PRIDE IN BEING A GOD OF THIEVES...

...IF I DIDN'T STEAL THAT BIKE.

CHAPTER 16

DARE! DELIVERY PICKUP AT THE GREAT DIVIDE SPORTING STORE.

I'M ON IT!

TIME TO RIDE!
AND... TIME FOR KARAOKE!

I GOT TO PUT ON... MY BOOGIE OOGIE SHOES!
KC & THE SUNSHINE BAND: TERRIBLY WARBLING REMIX

CLEAN UP THE DOG DOO!
POOP BAG
OH BOY OH YEAH. THEM GOOD OL' BOOGIE OOGIE SHOES.
WARG! WARG! BARK!
WARG! WARG!
H2O
FORGOT LYRICS, BUT CAN'T STOP, WON'T STOP.

WOW, EVERYONE'S A CRITIC.
WARG! WARG BUH-ROO!

BUT I HAVE A RULE THAT I DON'T TAKE CRITICISM FROM MEN WHO SAY "WELL, ACTUALLY..."
OR FROM ANYONE WHO POOPS ON EVERYTHING.
BORK!
H2O

CLEAN UP THE DOG DOO!
POOP BAG
H2O

CLEAN UP THE DOG DOO!
CHUCK. THE GOD OF THIEVES (ONE OF MANY)
SPOIKK!
!
AH-HAH!

THIS BIKE! SO POWERFUL! SO SLEEK! SO...MAGIC! IT MUST BE MINE!
?

THESE CHAINS ARE NO MATCH FOR SOMEONE WITH MY SKILLS, HONED OVER TENS OF THOUSANDS OF YEARS-
BARK BARK BARK BARK!!
POOP BAGS

OH, SHUT UP, WILL YOU?!
BARK BARK WARG GRRR BARK!

I STEAL YOUR VOICE!
WARG WARG BARK BA- ......
I STEAL YOUR FUR!
FLOOP!

NEVER MESS WITH THE GODS, HOUND.
WE ALWAYS GROW...ANGRY.
AND NOW, BACK TO THE BICYCLE, WHICH-

HUH?
IT'S GONE!
CLEAN UP THE DOG DOO!
POOP BAGS

GRETA! WE RIDE!
NO!

NOT REALLY ALL THAT FAR AWAY...

THERE HE IS.
TROT TROT TROT

AND THERE'S DARE!

ERRRRTTT!

PARK
TALL PIG!
DON'T CALL ME THAT, AND DON'T TALK IN PUBLIC, AND WHY ARE YOU HERE?!
IN STREET.
IN TROUBLE.

I CAME BECAUSE YOU HAVE A NEW DELIVERY!

NUDGE!
IT'S A MAGICALLY BOXED SLAP.

A... WHAT NOW?
MAGICALLY BOXED SLAP.
YOU JUST DELIVER IT TO THE RIGHT GOD, IT POPS OPEN, AND...
POW!
IT SLAPS THE HECK OUT OF 'EM.
WON'T THIS CAUSE TROUBLE?
OH YEAH. LOADS. BUT THAT'S NOT MY PROBLEM.
IT IS YOURS, THOUGH. LIKE, TOTALLY YOUR PROBLEM.

DARE! YOU FOUND THE PIG!

OH GEEZ. BE COOL. NO TALKING.

YEAH, HEY LULU. I FOUND THIS TOTALLY NORMAL PIG.
HI. I'M MOTORPOOL

GREAT TO MEET YOU, BUT... THIS...IS...A... **DELIVERY PIG!**
I MEAN, IT'S A PIG I HAVE TO **DELIVER!**
SO, I'LL JUST GO DO THAT, AND YOU'LL **NEVER EVER** SEE HIM AGAIN!

BYE!
BTS
WHOOSH!
TROT TROT
HOP TROT

OKAY I'M GONNA NEED HER PHONE NUMBER.

OSCAR WILDE
KARAOKETIME

CHAPTER 17

FELDANA.
LAND OF THE GODS.

DARE CRILLEY.
HUMAN BIKE MESSENGER.

PACKAGE TO BE DELIVERED.
CONTENTS: ONE RUDE SLAP.

POSSIBLE CONSEQUENCES OF DELIVERING A SLAP TO A GOD INCLUDE...
SMALK!

ELECTRIC RETRIBUTION.
VORE.
ETERNAL IMPRISONMENT.
HUH? HOW DID I GROW A **BEARD**?
TOTAL FORGIVENESS, AND A SLICE OF BLUEBERRY PIE.
THIS ONE SEEMS UNLIKELY.

CONSEQUENCES OF NOT DELIVERING PACKAGE ARE...
GODS AT WAR AND ULTIMATE DESTRUCTION OF ENTIRE MULTIVERSE, MAKING PIE EVEN MORE UNLIKELY.
WEIGHT ON DARE'S SHOULDERS: ELEVENTY JILLION POUNDS.

THAT'S THE BIKE I WAS TALKING ABOUT.
CHUCK: GOD OF THIEVES. (ONE OF MANY)
CHAD: GOD OF MANSCAPING.

I WAS TRICKED BEFORE, BUT I HAVE PLANS. HER APARTMENT IS BASICALLY OPEN TO ALL COMERS. SIMPLE LOCKS. SECOND FLOOR WINDOWS. NO ALARMS.
MOST OF THE DAY THERE'S NOTHING MORE THAN A CAT IN RESIDENCE.

THAT BIKE **WILL** BE MINE.
OKAY.

HEY, DO YOU HAVE A CURLING IRON?

BOUNCE
BOUNCE
DRIBBLE

SWOOSH!

HOLD UP, GUYS. BIKE COMING.

ROLL
ROLL
ROLL

FOOOM!

HELLO? UMM... IS YOUR NAME SHUGRA?
YES?
I HAVE A PACKAGE FOR YOU, BUT-

OH GOOD! A SURPRISE PACKAGE! I WONDER WHO-
NO! WAIT! DON'T OPEN IT! I WANTED TO EXPLAIN THAT-

IT'S A SLAP.
OOF!
WHOMP!
UMM...I HESITATE TO ASK, BUT...WHAT ARE YOU THE GOD OF?
I'M THE GOD OF UNDERSTANDING.
OH GOOD.
BUT I AM ALSO...
SPIN

...THE GOD OF RETRIBUTION.
OH. BAD. THAT'S VERY BAD.

RING
RING
RING

UHH, MIND IF I GET THIS?
SPIN
RING
RING
IT'S OKAY. WEIRD TIMING, BUT I UNDERSTAND.

HELLO? DARE?

IT'S MOTORPOOL. WE MET THE OTHER DAY? I'M LULU'S FRIEND. THE REALLY HOT ONE?

REKT
RE
PAR
LISTEN, STRAIGHT TO THE POINT. YOU WANNA GO OUT SOMETIME?
LIKE, I MEAN ON A FOR-REAL DATE?

A DATE?
YEP. DINNER. A WALK. WE PET EVERY DOG WE SEE.
STEAL A MOTORCYCLE AND RAMP OVER A SWIMMING POOL. THAT SORT OF THING.

YES. SOUNDS FUN.
COOL. I WISH YOU COULD SEE HOW MUCH I'M SMILING RIGHT NOW.
METAL G-L
MET
GHOST
GHOST
I'LL TEXT YOU DETAILS LATER, OKAY?

GREAT. BYE!
CLICK!

UH, SORRY ABOUT THE INTERRUPTION.
S'COOL. NO PROBLEM. I'M VERY UNDERSTANDING.

THAT'S **SUCH** A RELIEF! I WAS WORRIED THAT-
SPIN
WHAT I MEANT IS, I'M VERY UNDERSTANDING THAT...

!
CRACK!
...SOMEBODY'S ABOUT TO GET THEIR **ASS KICKED.**

CHAPTER 18

BEFORE ANY CARNAGE, I'D LIKE TO POINT OUT THAT I'M NOT THE ONE WHO ACTUALLY SENT YOU THE SLAP.
I'M JUST THE MESSENGER! NOT THE MESSAGE!

I KNOW. I TOTALLY UNDERSTAND.
I'M THE GOD OF UNDERSTANDING, REMEMBER?
SPIN
WHEW.

BUT WHEN I FIND OUT WHO'S RESPONSIBLE...
SPIN

...I'M THE GOD OF RETRIBUTION.

SEE YOU LATER, OKAY?
UH, OKAY, BYE.

WOW, THAT WAS A CLOSE ONE.
I'D BETTER-

WHOMP!
GUH!

?
SPLASH!

OOF!
THUMP!
AGGH!
THUMP!
GUH!

OH, COME ON! THERE WAS STILL A SLAP IN THERE?
THAT'S NOT FAIR!
SKRRT!

ONE HOUR LATER

WONDER WHAT THIS IS? BUT, YOU KNOW WHAT? I'M TOO TIRED TO CARE.
SPOOK

FLUMP!

GROSS. THE SHEETS SMELL LIKE *JUNG.*
LIKE, TOBACCO WITH A SMIRK. OR A SMUG FART.
I'M NEVER GOING TO GET TO SLEEP WITH HIS SMELL IN THE AIR.

zZZ
-SNORE-
Zzzzz

SNORE
ZURRK
Zzzzz

zzzZZZz
SNORFF...
Zzzzzzz
BEEP!
The only CAR I want is...
DARE! IT'S MOTORPOOL. I'LL PICK YOU UP IN THREE HOURS. LOOKING FORWARD TO SEEING YOU!

ssSSNORK!
zZZzz
Zzzzz
BAP
BAP BAP

YOU'RE LOOKING HAPPY.
NYOOOC

SURE AM, JIRBIL. I'VE GOT A BIG DATE TONIGHT. THAT DARE WOMAN. THE BICYCLE MESSENGER.
OOO! THAT MEANS STRONG LEGS! SEND ME A PICTURE OF HER TONIGHT!

NO. GROSS. BUT OKAY FOR SURE I WILL.

HMM.

CRIME
NOPE.
NOPE.
JUI CY
NOPE.

SABATON
OKAY. STAY COOL. STAY NORMAL.
AND QUIT DREAMING ABOUT KISSING HER.
BUT WEAR YOUR BEST UNDERWEAR, JUST IN CASE.

SNOZZLE
ZZZZZZ
SNORK

DARE'S PLACE!
707
WHEW. OKAY. HERE GOES.

KNOCK
KNOCK
KNOCK

KNOCK
KNOCK
KNOCK
??

WHO ARE YOU?

CHAPTER 19

KNOCK!
KNOCK!
KNOCK!

OH, CRAP! I SLEPT ALL DAY?! I'M SUCH AN IDIOT!
8:12

SMIRKLEY. SERIOUS DISCUSSION HERE. WHAT GOOD ARE YOU IN THIS WORLD?
YOU SHOULD HAVE WOKEN ME UP!

OKAY. FIRST THINGS FIRST. I NEED FRESH CLOTHES.
I SWEAT-SWAMPED THESE SO THEY HAVE TO-
KNOCK
KNOCK
KNOCK!

HUH?
THAT NEW MAGIC THINGY?
HOW'D IT GET ON **ME**?
URF!
AGH!
GUH!

IT WON'T COME OFF?
OKAY... GOTTA GET SOME COOKING OIL. GREASE UP MY FINGER. SLIDE THIS WEIRD RING RIGHT OFF.
WHO **KNOWS** WHAT THIS THING DOES?
THUMP
THUMP
THUMP!

KNOCK!
KNOCK!
KNOCK!

SHE'S NOT ANSWERING. AND... I HAVE A DATE WITH HER.
NOT SURE WHY YOU'RE HERE.
FOR RETRIBUTION.

...FOR WHAT NOW?
I AM A GOD, AND I WILL NOT WAIT FOR A HUMAN TO ANSWER THE DOOR.

OPEN!

OH.
OH HI.
SABATON

I UNDERSTAND THAT I HAVE DONE WRONG.
YEP.
SABATON
DARE CRILLEY, I WANTED TO TELL YOU THAT I'VE TRACKED DOWN THE ORIGINAL SENDER OF THE PACKAGE. A GOD NAMED JUNG.
I WILL BE SERVING RETRIBUTION.
GOOD. FANTASTIC. KINDA FEELING EXPOSED RIGHT NOW, THOUGH. CAN I GET A MOMENT?

HEY DARE. I'M HERE FOR OUR DATE. YOU LOOK NICE. NEW MAKEUP?
KINDA FEELING LIKE WE'RE ALL OVER-LOOKING HOW I'M NAKED, HERE.

I'M... JUST GONNA BE RIGHT BACK.

thapp!
MEWR!
SLAPP!
JUICY

CAN YOU EVEN CONCEIVE OF HOW MANY DIFFERENT WAYS I'M GOING TO MURDER YOU?

OKAY. GRABBED A QUICK SHOWER. GOT DRESSED.
GOOD UNDERWEAR BECAUSE, YOU KNOW, JUST IN CASE. AND...

HMM.

OKAY. ONE QUICK JAUNT TO FELDANA.
JUNG'S A TOTAL JERK, BUT IF THE GOD OF RETRIBUTION IS AFTER HIM, HE DESERVES A WARNING.

CLICK!

VOOOP!
HEY. SORRY TO BUG YOU. ANYONE SEEN JUNG?

SEEN JUNG?

HI. ANYONE SEEN JUNG?
1/2
1

OKAY, I TRIED, BUT... TIMES UP.
I'VE GOT A HOT DATE.
fizzle
A.M.

OKAY! READY TO GO?
YEP! AND... WOW! YOU LOOK GREAT EVEN WITH CLOTHES ON.
SABATON

FORBIDDEN TOPIC, MOTORPOOL.
YOU'LL SOON LEARN THAT THERE ARE NO FORBIDDEN TOPICS ON A DATE WITH ME.

CLICK!

VOOP!
?

farewell Smirkley...

CHAPTER 20

I'VE HEARD THAT IF YOU PET ONE HUNDRED DOGS IN A SINGLE DAY, YOU GET TO MAKE A WISH.
IT'S SORT OF LIKE RUBBING A GENIE'S LAMP, EXCEPT IN THIS CASE THE GENIE IS A DOG.

ALSO, YOUR FIRST TWO WISHES HAVE TO BE ABOUT BELLY RUBS AND NAPS.
SABATON
THEY WOULD'VE BEEN ANYWAY.

HOW MANY DOGS HAVE WE PETTED SO FAR TONIGHT?
SEVEN.
ONLY NINETY-THREE TO GO. SHOULD WE FORTIFY OURSELVES WITH...

NINE MINUTES LATER...

TEMPORARY TIMEOUT ON OUR SEARCH FOR DOGS, AND THE QUEST FOR WISHES.
CHOCOLATE ABOMINATION.
STRAIGHT WHISKEY.
BENT WHISKEY.
PINEAPPLE PARAMOUR.
SABATON

YOU KNOW, IF THIS WAS AN RPG, I FEEL LIKE WE'D BE LEVELING UP SOON.
I LOVE DATING SIMS.
EXCEPT THE ONES THAT DON'T LET YOU SLEEP WITH EVERYONE.
SABATON

YOU'RE RIGHT. THOSE AREN'T FAIR.
BUT, NOW THAT WE'RE BOOZED UP AND OUR INHIBITIONS ARE DECIMATED,
LET'S FIND OUT ABOUT EACH OTHER!
WHAT DO YOU WHAT DO KNOW?
SABATON

WEIRD STUFF. LIKE, WHO'S THE GROSSEST PERSON YOU STILL WANT TO KISS?
WOULD YOU RATHER BE A WEREWOLF, A VAMPIRE, OR A WITCH?
AND, WHAT'S THE STUPIDEST PLACE YOU EVER PEED?
SABATON

ELSEWHERE...
NNNNH...
JUNG! IT'S BURNING! IT'S BURNING! I'M...
...I'M BURNING!!!
YOU SHOULD HAVE SAVED ME.
YOU SHOULD HAVE SAVED ME!!!
...I THOUGHT YOU LOVED ME...

AHHHH!

THE DREAM, AGAIN?
...
WHAT ARE YOU DOING IN MY APARTMENT?

CAME TO DISCUSS CATS WITH YOU.

THIS ONE IN PARTICULAR.
IT'S DARE'S CAT. JUNG.
YOU STOLE HER CAT.

OF COURSE I STOLE HER CAT. IT'S MY HOSTAGE.
I'M GOING TO USE IT TO EXPOSE DARE FOR WHAT SHE IS. **AN EVIL HUMAN.**

DARE'S NOT EVIL.
WELL, I SAY SHE IS.

WHAT IF YOU'RE WRONG?

WHAT IF I DON'T CARE IF I'M WRONG?

WHAT IF I DON'T CARE?

NEW RULE!
WHOEVER SEES THE NEXT DOG FIRST GETS TO KISS THE OTHER PERSON!
SOUNDS LIKE I GET A KISS EITHER WAY.
YEAH, THE GAME IS RIGGED.
FINE BY ME.

MEANWHILE...

oh no...

CHAPTER 21

MOTORPOOL, THIS HAS BEEN... AN AMAZING FIRST DATE.
SABATON

SO, WOULD YOU LIKE TO COME INSIDE FOR A BIT?

YEAH! THAT WOULD BE-

NO!

HUH?
OH. UH. CRAP. I... UM.

LOOK. I DON'T WANT TO RUIN ANYTHING. I THINK WE SHOULD TAKE THINGS SLOW.
NEXT DATE'S ON ME, OKAY?
OH. OKAY?
KISS!
BYE.
WAVE WAVE...
SLAM!

TORGA! WHY ARE YOU HERE?
I WAS ON A DATE!
AND I WANTED TO TAKE THINGS FAST!

JUNG STOLE YOUR CAT.
ONE OF THE GODS OF THIEVES STOLE YOUR BIKE.

blink
blink

WELL. HERE'S A MOOD SWING.

GRAHHH!

MY CAT!
KICK!

TOSS!
TOSS!
MY BIKE!

SWORD!
JUNG IS A JERK!

HUH?
WHERE'D I GET THIS **SWORD**?
HMM.
YOUR HAND. THAT RING.
THAT'S A LEVEL 98 SWORD SUMMONER.
HUH? EXPLAIN.
"ANYTIME YOU'RE WEARING THAT, YOU CAN SUMMON A POWERFUL SWORD. THE DEVICE WAS SUPPOSED TO ATTACH TO YOUR BIKE, BUT IT CLAMPED ONTO YOU FOR SOME REASON."
HMM.

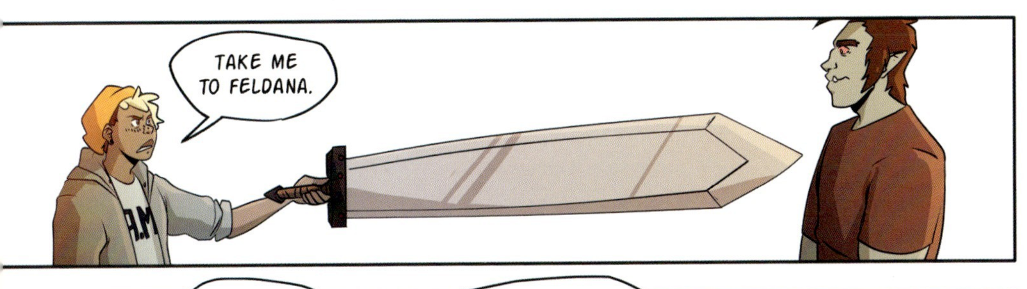
TAKE ME TO FELDANA.

SURE. BUT ONLY BECAUSE JUNG DESERVES THIS. NOT BECAUSE YOU'RE THREATENING ME.
VOOP!

BECAUSE, DARE CRILLEY, YOU'D BEST HEED ME, HERE. I **DON'T** THREATEN WELL.
AND, REMEMBER... I'M THE GOD OF INTERNET SEARCH HISTORY.

REMEMBER LAST TUESDAY?
YOUR SEARCH FOR "WEREWOLVES WITH BIG-"

POINT TAKEN!
I'M SORRY I WAS MEAN.
BUT WE **ARE** GOING TO FELDANA.

YOU HAVE ANY IDEA WHERE JUNG IS AT?
NONE. WE'LL HAVE TO ASK AROUND.

CAN DO.

ANY OF YOU DEERMAIDS KNOW WHERE JUNG IS AT?

DRAG!
HEY **YOU!**
HAVE YOU SEEN MY **BIKE?**

ANY OF YOU KNOW WHERE THE GODS OF THIEVES HANG OUT?

HOW MUCH FOR THESE CUPCAKES?

ANY OF YOU KNOW WHERE-?
HEY!

HUH? SHUGRA?
DARE DALT CRILLEY. I HAVE HEARD YOUR FELINE AND YOUR BICYCLE WERE STOLEN.
I'M GUESSING YOU'RE LOOKING FOR...

RETRIBUTION.

YUP.

TEAM-UP!

CHAPTER 22

OKAY. I'M TEAMED UP WITH THE GOD OF RETRIBUTION AND THE GOD OF INTERNET BROWSING HISTORY.
SO THAT'S GOOD.
I'M ACTUALLY JUST OBSERVING.
A.M!

FIRST, WE NEED TO FIND EITHER THAT GOD OF THIEVES, CHUCK OR THE GOD OF SUPER STUPID JERKS, JUNG.
ANY IDEAS WHERE THEY MIGHT BE?

I KNOW EXACTLY WHERE THEY ARE.
A.M!

OH. HUH. OKAY.
WELL, THAT MAKES THINGS EASIER.

SOON...

SLOOT!

HAH! THE BICYCLE IS WHERE THE LIKES OF **YOU** DON'T HAVE **ANY** CHANCE OF GETTING IT, HUMAN!

"IT'S SUSPENDED OVER AN OPEN CALDERA OF BOILING LAVA, ATTACHED BY A LEVEL 97 THIEF ROPE, SO GOOD LUCK EVER..."

A.M!

ROUTE PLANNED.

LEAP!

MY PIE!
RUN RUN RUN

JUMP
THUMP

A.M!
SWORD!
SLICE!
GOT YOU, GRETA!
GRAB!

FALL!
DARE! THE LAVA!
CLICK!
PORTAL!
PLUNGE!

FWOMP!
!

OH, HI, MOTORPOOL.
A.M!
DARE?

YEAH, BUT... AHH... YOU'RE DREAMING!
YOU FELL ASLEEP IN THE TUB. I'M NOT REALLY HERE.
A.M!

SMOOCH!

PORTAL!

WHERE'D THAT MORTAL GO? INTO THE LAVA?
DID THE HUMAN DIE IN THE...?
HER NAME IS DARE, AND...

SHE'S BEHIND YOU.
A.M!
DON'T EVER STEAL MY BICYCLE AGAIN.
RIGHT NOW I ADMIT TO SOME REGRETS.

ELSEWHERE...

CHAPTER 23

SO YOU WENT ON A DATE WITH DARE, AND THEN HAD SOME WEIRD BATHTUB DREAM ABOUT HER?
George's
P4
P5
THAT'S THE SIZE OF IT.

BEST WE DON'T HEAR ALL THE DETAILS. TOM HAS A HUGE CRUSH ON DARE.
OH! I'M SORRY.

S'OKAY. IT'S NOT LIKE I WAS IN LOVE WITH HER OR ANYTHING.
I MEAN, I'M NOT HAVING ANY BATHTUB HALLUCINATIONS OR ANYTHING.

DREAMS AREN'T HALLUCINATIONS.
I'M SMITTEN. NOT INSANE.
RIP

INSANITY IS UNDER-RATED, MOTORPOOL. IF I WERE YOU, I'D GO ALL IN.

I'D LIKE A SLICE OF CARROT CAKE AND... OH, A LEMONADE.
RIP

AND MY FRIEND TOM IS HEARTBROKEN. WHAT'S GOOD FOR A BROKEN HEART?
TRIPLE SHOT, DOUBLE PUMP, MOCHA.

AND THIS BLUEBERRY-FILLED QUADRUPLE CHOCOLATE MUFFIN.
FROM HEARTBREAK TO HEART ATTACK SOUNDS GREAT.

C'MON, MY PLACE IS CLOSE BY. WE'LL HANG THERE FOR A WHILE.
RIP

CLICK!
HEY, JIRBIL. BROUGHT SOME FRIENDS OVER.
I'M LULU. THIS SAD LOOKING ONE IS TOM.

WHAT'S HE SAD ABOUT?
WOMEN TROUBLES.
HERE I AM. RIGHT HERE.

HE SEEMS CUTE ENOUGH. HE HAVE ANY MUSCLES? BRAINS?
A LITTLE OF BOTH. MORE OF THE BRAINS.

HMM. EMPLOYED?
HE'S A PUBLISHER. HAS HIS OWN COMPANY.

BAD BREATH? BAD MANNERS? BAD FARTS?
NOPE. NOPE. AND THANKFULLY UNKNOWN.

AH, HE'LL BE FINE, THEN.
YEAH, THAT'S WHAT I KEEP TELLING HIM.
IS THERE A CORNER I CAN HIDE IN?

SO, WE HAVE A DECISION.
IS THIS THE TYPE OF GATHERING WHERE WE SIT AROUND WITH COFFEE AND PASTRIES DISCUSSING LIFE AND ART AND ALL THAT?

OR IS IT THE SAME THING, BUT WITH BOOZE?
YES, BOOZE PLEASE.
BOOZE.
BOOZE.

THE GOOD STUFF
IT'S RUM!

SO LET ME GET THIS STRAIGHT.
MOTORPOOL, YOU'RE GOING OUT WITH DARE. TOM, YOU WANTED TO BUT SHE IGNORED YOU?
I WOULDN'T SAY "IGNORED."
RIP

I WOULD, TOM.
AND I WAS THERE!
OOPSIE! THAT WAS CRASS. MAYBE I'VE HAD TOO MUCH BOOZE.
NAW. I LIKE HONEST PEOPLE.

AND PLUS YOU'RE KINDA ADORABLE AS A CRASS DRUNK.
RIP

I'M GONNA TEXT DARE!
RIP
SORRY

WE ALL PROMISE NOT TO LOOK IF YOU'RE WANTING TO SEND NUDES.
RIP
SORRY
I'M NOT SENDING HER ANY NUDES!

WAIT. DO YOU THINK I SHOULD?

RIP
SORRY
WHOA. SLOW DOWN.
NO NUDES UNTIL THE SECOND DATE.

OKAY. OKAY, BUT I'M GONNA ASK HER OUT AGAIN.
WHERE DO YOU THINK WE SHOULD GO? WHAT'S SHE LIKE TO DO?
RIP
SORRY

HMM. WHAT'S SHE LIKE TO DO?
WELL, SOMETHING ACTIVE, I'D SAY, BECAUSE...

"DARE LIKES TO BE ACTIVE."
A.M!

SMIRKLEY! I'M COMING FOR YOU!
A.M!

CAW
CAW
SWISH!
CAW

CAW
CAW
CAW
CAW
A.M!
CAW
CAW

CHAPTER 24

SEVERAL THOUSAND YEARS AGO.
FELDANA.
THE LAND OF GODS.

JUNG, DID YOU LEAVE THESE FLOWERS FOR ME?
OF COURSE NOT, MARADA. ONLY SOMEONE DEEPLY IN LOVE WITH YOU WOULD DO SUCH A THING.

I SEE. I WONDER WHERE THE CULPRIT IS, THEN?
IF I WERE YOU, I'D LOOK ELSEWHERE.

I WOULD LOOK BENEATH THE SEAS.

OR BEHIND THE RAINBOWS.

I WOULD ASK THE WIND TO WHISPER THE TRUTH.

I WILL DO NONE OF THESE THINGS.
INSTEAD, I WILL SIMPLY KNOW, BEYOND TRUTH, THAT YOU LEFT THE FLOWERS FOR ME.

I'LL NOT ARGUE.
IT'S A FOOL WHO ARGUES WITH A BEAUTIFUL WOMAN.

IT'S A FOOL WHO DOESN'T, YOU MEAN. WE BEAUTIFUL WOMEN HAVE MORE THAN ENOUGH PEOPLE TO AGREE WITH US.
WHERE'S THE FUN IN THAT?

OH HO! YOU'RE PROCLAIMING YOURSELF BEAUTIFUL, THEN?
WHAT ARROGANCE!

OF COURSE I THINK I'M BEAUTIFUL!
AND I DIDN'T NEED THE SEAS OR ANY RAINBOWS OR THE WIND TO CONVINCE ME.

BECAUSE I SEE ENOUGH OF THAT TRUTH IN YOUR EYES, JUNG.

JUNG!

TORGA? GO AWAY!
SORRY, JUNG! SORRY, MARADA! BUT...

...THERE'S A HUMAN IN FELDANA.

A WHAT? AND, WHO CARES?
MAKE IT GO AWAY!

WE WILL!
BUT FIRST, I'M AFRAID THE HUMAN ANGERED SIDRA!

"SHE'S GONE CRAZY! HER FLAMES ARE EVERYWHERE!"

CAN YOU TALK TO HER? CALM HER DOWN? YOU'RE THE GOD OF MEADOWS AND STREAMS.
IF ANYONE CAN BRING SOME SERENITY TO-

LOOK OUT!
WHOOOOSH!

FWOOMM!

NO!

MARADA!

JUNG! YOU CAN'T GO IN THERE!
LET ME GO! MY WIFE IS IN THERE!
MARADA!

SKRITCH!

FELDANA, TODAY...
SLASH!

A.M
SWOOSH!
SLASH!

HUFF!
A.M!

JUNG! YOU'RE GOING TO MAKE ME **MAD!**
I **KNOW** YOU HAVE SMIRKLEY, AND I'M GOING TO-

THAPP!
MWRRR!

THUMPPP!

DAMN IT, SMIRKLEY. SOMETIMES YOU ARE THE WORST.

THUMP!

OKAY, HUMAN. YOU WANT TO FIGHT A GOD?

HERE'S YOUR CHANCE.

CHAPTER 25

DING!
FIGHT!
MAGICAL GESTURE!
NAPKIN!
MORE NAPKINS!

VVVVOOM!

PAPER NAPKIN GOLEM

HIT POINTS: 107
ALIGNMENT: NEUTRAL
ATTACK: 9TH LEVEL. (+5 MODIFIER)
SPEED: 10

ER NAPKIN
POINTS: 107
NMENT: NEUTRAL
ACK: 9TH LEVEL.
EED: 10
GOLEM
+5 MODIFIER)
SLICE!

YOU BROUGHT PAPER NAPKINS TO A SWORD FIGHT?
A.M!

THE GODS MUST BE CRAZY.

YOU'LL QUIT MOCKING THE GODS WHEN YOU SEE HOW POWERFUL-

OOF!
WHUMPP!
YOU'LL QUIT MOCKING ME WHEN YOU FEEL HOW POWERFUL MY LEGS ARE!

GAHH!
THUMP!
THESE LEGS CAN PEDAL A BIKE FOR DAYS!
SO THEY CAN **CERTAINLY** KICK BUTT ON A CAT-STEALING NAPKIN-BABY!
A.M!

SHOULD WE DO SOMETHING?
PERSONALLY, I THINK NOT.
PLUS I'M AFRAID OF THAT SWORD.

YEAH. IT'S A BIG SWORD.

HMM. DON'T YOU RECOGNIZE IT?

RECOGNIZE IT?
NO. SHOULD I?

SHOULD YOU, HMM?
GOOD QUESTION. HMM.

NOW YOU'VE DONE IT.
NOW YOU'VE DONE IT!
YOU'VE ANGERED ME, HUMAN! AND NO HUMAN WILL EVER-

HSSSST!

GONNNG!

!
?

WELL, THAT'S A NEW DELIVERY NOTICE.

I HAVE TO DO THIS IMMEDIATELY.
FIGHT'S OVER.

THE FATE OF THE UNIVERSE JUST SAVED YOU.

C'MON SMIRKLEY. LET'S GET YOU HOME.

OH GEEZE. LOOK AT THIS.
I HAVE TO DELIVER A **BABY ELEPHANT?**

HOW AM I GONNA DO THAT?

SHE'S LUCKY FOR THE INTERRUPTION.
WRONG.

YOU WERE GETTING YOUR ASS KICKED.
AND BY A PAIR OF REALLY NICE LEGS, AS DARE POINTED OUT.

HELLO! WHAT'S THIS?
DO I DETECT A LITTLE-
...

SHE ACTUALLY DOES HAVE NICE LEGS.

!
SLAP!!!
UNGG!

RETRIBUTION!

ELSEWHERE...

TOM OL' BOY. YOU'VE DONE IT.
DID YOU SEE THE WAY LULU BLUSHED?
YES SIR. I THINK SHE LIKES YOU.
BRUSH!
BRUSH!
AND SHE'S AMAZING.
THINGS ARE DEFINITELY LOOKING UP! THINGS ARE-

FWUMPP!

AHHHHHHHH!!

TO BE CONTINUED...

GALLERY

COVER ART

MOTION TRIPTYCH

DUSTJACKET ART